THREE DAYS TO CATCH THE KILLER!

DKA agency (automobile repossessions) had a slightly more serious matter on its hands. Bart Heslip, one of its best detectives, was lying in the hospital with a cracked skull after pulling in a Jag and a Montego.

The docs gave Heslip 72 hours. The boss gave Larry Ballard just as long to find the guy who did it.

Ballard hit the case hard. Driven beyond endurance, he worked day and night. And in a blind rage he stumbled onto the real thing . . . Murder One!

Dead Skip

Joe Gores

BALLANTINE BOOKS • NEW YORK

Library of Congress Catalog Card Number: 72-5403

ISBN 0-345-29206-5

This edition published by arrangement with
Random House, Inc.

Manufactured in the United States of America

First Ballantine Books Edition: August 1974
Second Printing: March 1981

This one is for
Dave Kikkert,
who lives it every day,
and for
Tony Boucher and Fred Dannay

Dead
Skip

One

The 1969 Plymouth turned into Seventh Avenue from Fulton, away from Golden Gate Park. It was a quiet residential neighborhood in San Francisco's Richmond District—white turning black, with a sprinkling of Chinese. The Plymouth went slowly; its brights picked out a couple of FOR SALE signs on narrow two- and three-story buildings. It was just midnight.

In midblock, the lone man behind the wheel saw a 1972 Mercury Montego hardtop parked directly across from the closed Safeway supermarket. He whistled thinly through his teeth. "Yeah, man," he said softly, "squatting right on the address."

He parked around the corner. From his clipboard he selected a sheet of paper with several pink report carbons stapled to the back of it, folded it into thirds, and slid it into his inside jacket pocket. From beneath the dash he unhinged a magnetic flashlight; from the glove box he took a hot wire, a ring of filed-down keys, and two oddly bent steel hooks.

The heavy rubber soles of his garage attendant's shoes made no sound on the sidewalk. By the street lights he was very black, with a wide flared nose and a thin mustache and an exaggerated breadth of shoulder which made him look much heavier than his 158 pounds.

The Montego was locked.

As he shone his flashlight through the window on the driver's side, a head appeared behind the white lace curtain in the central bay window at 736. If the black

1

man saw it, he gave no indication. The face disappeared abruptly; moments later the recessed front door opened to spill a bulky shadow out across the steps.

"Hey, you! Get to hell away from that car!"

When the other man did not comply, he came cautiously down the steps on stockinged feet. He had a round pale face and wavy brown receding hair.

The black finally looked at him. "Are you the owner of this car, sir?"

"Yeah, what the hell busi—"

"Are you Harold J. Willets?" he persisted. He had to refer to his sheet of paper for the name, even though it was not a new assignment. He thought in terms of autos and licenses and addresses, not names.

"Yeah," said Willets again, edging closer to see the paper.

The black man nodded briskly, like a doctor whose diagnosis has just been confirmed by the x-rays. "Yes, sir. My name is Barton Heslip, I have a repossession order for your Mercury."

"A repossession order? For *my* car?"

"A legal order from the bank, yes, sir. Could I have the keys, please?"

"No, you can't have the keys, please," mimicked Willets. He had gained confidence in talking. "And you can't have the car. You go tell the bank you couldn't find it. *Wouldn't* have found it if the garage lock hadn't been busted."

Heslip was not surprised; he had broken off a toothpick in the lock earlier that evening, hoping that Willets would leave the car in the street when the garage key would not work. He had been trying to catch the car outside the garage for a week.

"What is it, Harry?" A woman had appeared at the head of the steps. She wore a faded pink terry-cloth robe and woolly slippers.

To Heslip, Willets said, "You can go to hell," to his wife, "This ni—this guy says he's from the bank, wants to take my car."

"*What?*" Outrage shrilled in her voice. She pattered

down the steps, hair in curlers and face cold-creamed. "He can't do that. Harry, you tell him he can't do that." Heslip sighed: wives were a drag. She went on, seeing the repossession order in his hand, "You said the bank. Who's this Daniel Kearny Associates?"

"We're an investigation agency employed by the bank, ma'am."

"We never got no notice or anything—"

"You're three payments delinquent tomorrow," he said patiently. "No bank would let an account get that far down without notification. Besides, *you* knew you hadn't made the payments."

"Well, you can't have the car," said Willets. "Mae took the payments into the bank just today."

"Then you'll have the cashier's stamp in your payment book."

Mae cast an angry glance at her husband. "I . . . mailed them in."

"Then I'll look at the check stub."

"I—I sent cash," she said desperately. "Just the cash money."

"Uh-huh." Heslip's voice became suddenly, savagely scornful. "You just stuck a rubber band around three one-hundred-dollar bills and threw them into the mailbox." He turned to Willets. "Are there any personal possessions you'd like to remove from the car?"

Willets moved his stockinged feet around on the damp sidewalk as if belatedly realizing they were cold. It was a crisp spring night with just a touch of ocean wind and the vaguest hint of mist. "I lost the keys," he said complacently.

Heslip shrugged. He took one of the steel hooks from his pocket, inserted it into the joint between the front and rear side windows, and gave a quick flick of a powerful wrist. The door was open.

"Hey, you black bastard!" yelped Willets, startled.

Heslip spun swiftly, skipping sideways to be free of the Montego's door. His eyes were black coals. Willets backed off hastily from the look on his face, his hands up placatingly.

"Don't you dare lay a hand on my husband!" Mae shrilled. "What kind of man are you, preying on decent folks—"

"I pay my bills," said Heslip. He was breathing harshly.

The white man's mouth was working. "Oh, to hell with you," he said suddenly. "Take the goddamn thing!" He jerked a bunch of keys from his pocket and threw them with all his might at the Mercury. They starred the driver's window with multiple fine fracture lines.

Heslip picked them up from the gutter. "What about your possessions?" His voice was even once more.

"That's your lookout—and they all better be there when I get that car back, or I'll sue your dead-beat company . . ."

His voice trailed off as he stamped up the brick-edged stairs. His wife followed, her back rigid with contempt and indignation. At the head of the stairs, with the front door open, Willets turned back. "Just what you'd expect from a nigger!" he yelled. Then he was inside behind Mae, slamming the door.

Heslip got into the Mercury, sat with his hands rigid on the wheel like a man in catalepsy. Finally the tension began leaving his features; he shrugged; he even grinned. "No class, baby," he said aloud.

It took only four minutes to park around the corner behind his company Plymouth and fasten his tow bar to the Mercury's front bumper. He left on the parking lights. Before starting off with his tow, he wrote the date and a few scrawled notes to himself on the face of the uppermost pink report carbon. These would form the raw data, later, for his typed report on the Willets assignment.

At Arguello, he unclipped his radio mike from the dash. "SF-3 calling SF-6. Do you read me, Larry?"

No response. At USF he took the linked cars over to Golden Gate, one-way inbound to the office, and tried again. This time he was successful. "How you doing, man?" he asked.

"Not a thing." The disgust in Larry Ballard's voice came through the mike clearly. "Haven't seen a car. You're having a good night."

Which meant Ballard had been by the office, had seen the two repos Heslip already had brought in.

"Got that Willets Merc on the tow bar right now."

"That toothpick in the lock actually work?"

"Like a charm, man. Willets don't like culluhed folks, but he gave me the keys. Where you at now?"

"Way out beyond Twin Peaks, up in those little streets off Ocean."

"I'll be 10-8 at the office, cat," said Heslip. "Got sixteen cases to type reports on. And I got something funny on one of the files. Probably just a coincidence, but I wanta ask what you think."

"10-4," said Ballard.

Heslip unlocked the chain-link storage lot under the concrete abutments of the skyway adjacent to the DKA office, unhooked the Mercury, and ran it in, then swiftly made out a condition report on a printed snap-out multiple form. This covered mileage, mechanical condition, lights, glass, body, rubber, power extras such as steering, seats, windows, brakes. He also checked the glove box, trunk, under the seats, on the back ledge, and behind the visors for personal property. Each item was meticulously noted, down to a box of Kleenex.

His thoroughness was professional and habitual, and owed nothing at all to Willets' threats. Threats were cheap in Heslip's business. He had started as a field agent with Daniel Kearny Associates three years before, when he had realized he wasn't going to be middleweight champ of the world after all; it was the only profession he knew which could give him the same one-on-one excitement he'd found in the ring.

After relocking the lot, Heslip let himself into the DKA basement and locked himself in. Along the left wall were the field agents' cubicles, each with a desk, two chairs, typewriter, phone, and a set of trays holding various forms necessary for the paper work. Along the right was a long bank of meshed cages; into one of them went the personal property he had removed from the Willets car. He patted the fender of the new Jaguar he'd picked up earlier. He'd put it in the garage instead of the lot because a car like that just seemed to attract the vandals.

When he dialed 553-1235 on the phone, a hard masculine voice came on with "Traffic Detail, Delaney."

"I've got a repo for you."

"Yeah, just a sec." Sound of paper-shuffling. "Okay. Shoot."

"Seventy-two Mercury Montego hardtop, blue in color, license 1-8-0, Baker-Eddie-Baker, motor number 1-9-7-2-M-3-6-9-7-0-8. Repo'd at Seventh Avenue and Cabrillo, registered owner—"

"Yeah, what time?"

"Oh." Heslip checked his watch. "Say . . . thirty-five, forty minutes ago. Make it twelve-twenty. Registered owner is Harold J-as-in-Joseph Willets, 7-3-6 Seventh Avenue. Legal is California Citizens Bank, San Francisco."

"Yeah, who's this?"

"Kearny Associates—Heslip. Busy downtown?"

"Sitting on our cans drinking coffee. At the moment."

"Think I'll be a cop so I can quit work."

"Wait until the bars close and they start running into each other. Them people probably give you the keys and buy you a beer besides."

"Sure they do."

The policeman laughed and repeated his name, adding his shield number, and hung up. Heslip wrote both on the face of the Willets case sheet so he could include them in his closing report. Sixteen of those mothers to write, take him damned near the rest of the night. That one case, probably just a coincidence, still . . . Maybe Larry would come up with an idea on it. He'd trained Ballard, two years ago; hell of a good man, had all the instincts. Except he got involved.

Reports, damn 'em. He turned to the typewriter, stopped. He'd left the case sheets folded in thirds up above his car visor; he always put them up there when they were ready for reports.

Still carrying the Willets case sheet in his hand, he let himself out into the cold night air, now wet and heavy with mist. As he started across Golden Gate toward the

Plymouth, a dark shape came out of the recessed entryway from which interior stairs led up to the main-floor clerical offices.

Heslip whirled around, was bringing up his guard when he was struck sharply above the right temple with a small truncheon. It made a nasty meaty sound against his skull. He went down on his hands and knees, one foot pawing the curb clumsily in a reflex to get upright inside the count. The truncheon swung again with panicky haste, struck an inch above the place it had hit the first time.

Heslip went down hard, on his face this time, without trying to break the fall in any way. He twitched once and was still.

Two

At 8:27 A.M. Larry Ballard parked his company Ford in front of the elementary school playground, yawned, and pulled a dozen folded case sheets from above his visor. Report-typing time. Erg.

Carrying them and the attaché case containing his *Current, Hold,* and *Contingent* folders, he locked the car and started across Golden Gate Avenue. A screaming phalanx of little black kids burst from the school into the blacktopped playground. His eye caught a fluttering beneath the windshield wiper of Heslip's Plymouth; grinning, he went back to feed his own meter. Then the grin faded. Odd that it would be parked in the same place it had been the night before, when he had come in at 1:25 and hadn't been able to find Bart.

On impulse he checked the basement before going upstairs to Clerical. The Jaguar that Bart had picked up last night was gone. Had it been gone at 1:25? He just hadn't noticed. Marty Rossman came out of his cubicle, tall and wavy-haired; he had never lived down once yelling "May Day! May Day!" over the car radio when four angry Samoan lads had started tipping over his car in the housing project out off Geneva Avenue.

"Bart Heslip down here, Marty?"

Rossman shook his head. "Haven't seen him. Kearny is taking off heads this morning."

"Hell, and I've got reports to write."

Ballard slipped back outside and then in the adjacent door to climb the narrow creaking stairs to the second

8

floor. In the 1920s this old charcoal Victorian which housed DKA (Head Office, San Francisco, Branch Offices in All Major California Cities) had been a specialty whorehouse; recently it had been designated a California Landmark by the State Historical Society. Such are the uses of fame.

At the head of the stairs he turned hard left, toward the front office which overlooked the avenue through unwashed bay windows. Two new assignments and five memos from the skip-tracers, as well as three close-outs, were in his box on Jane Goldson's desk.

"Bart up here, Jane?"

"No. Should he be?"

Jane was the setup and switchboard girl, with a marked English accent which Kearny felt lent the place a touch of class. He might even have been right. She also had remarkably good legs under remarkably short skirts; a slight open-faced girl with brown, perfectly straight hair all the way down to the small of her back.

"He's not downstairs and his car is outside. And the Jaguar he picked up last night is gone."

"Maybe he's taking it back to the dealer." She suddenly frowned. "He picked that one up, did he? Bit odd, actually, that he didn't leave a note on my desk about it."

Carrying his attaché case and the *In* basket contents, Ballard clattered downstairs and back into the basement. The sliding mirrored door at Kearny's cubbyhole at the far end was shut, but that didn't mean anything; it was one-way glass so Kearny could see who wanted in. Besides, Ballard was going to have to ask him if he'd seen Bart, no matter what sort of mood he was in.

Ballard's intercom rang before he could set down his attaché case. "Larry? Come in here right away."

Ballard walked back, pushed the button beside Kearny's door; when the buzzer sounded, he went in. Standing behind the desk, where she could read over Kearny's shoulder, was Giselle Marc. She still had on her coat: a tall, wickedly lean blonde with an exquisitely boned face and the sort of brains that traditionally go with thick horn-rims, thick ankles, and a thick personality. She had only the brains.

"I hear that Kathy's sick again," said Ballard, just to say something.

"She is. It worries me. She's too young for all the troubles she has." Kathy Onoda, the Japanese-American office manager, was just twenty-eight. Giselle was two years younger, the same age as Ballard.

He sat down in the client chair, gingerly, awaiting Kearny's eruption. All of the signs were there: Giselle, long-faced, unsmiling; the ashtray overflowing with half-smoked butts; Kearny's coat over the back of his chair; Kearny himself hunched forward in a watching attitude as if the Derby were being run on top of his desk.

Ballard cleared his throat. "Bart's got another ticket. Can't we do something about that new meter maid?"

"What time did you see Bart last night?" asked Kearny. He shook out a Lucky, offered the pack, regarding the younger man through the smoke with narrowed eyes.

"I didn't—just talked with him on the radio about twelve-thirty. He said he'd be here, writing reports—he had sixteen of 'em to do. But he was already gone when I got here at one-twenty-five."

"Was the Jag he repo'd here? Were the burglar alarms set?"

Ballard hesitated. Bart was his best friend; he didn't want to give wrong answers.

"Well?" Kearny was a hard-driving forty-four, a compact, blocky man with cop's eyes, a massive jaw, and a slightly flattened and bent nose which helped mask the cold shrewdness of his face. He had been a private investigator for over a quarter of a century, managing Walter's Auto Detectives, until he had founded DKA almost ten years before.

"I didn't notice about the Jag. The door was locked but the alarms were off. Why? What—"

"Bart's in the hospital," said Giselle.

"Hospital?" Ballard stood up abruptly, remained erect for several seconds, then with a slightly foolish look, sat down again.

"He creamed that Jaguar," said Kearny mildly.

"That's silly, Dan. He picked it up early in the evening, it was here when I was by at ten-thirty." He looked over at Giselle, who was leaning against the filing cabinet with her arms folded. "Is he hurt bad?"

"He *totaled* the goddamn Jag!" Kearny burst out. He slammed the desk so hard with an open palm that his dice box full of ballpoint pens jumped a full inch in the air. "One of the new V-12 hardtop coupes and he *totaled* it. Joy-riding like some damned teen-ager—"

"Bart wouldn't do that!" exclaimed Ballard hotly. "He—"

"Almost twelve thousand owing on it—hell, we picked it up because the subject's insurance had been canceled. Our insurance is probably primary over the bank's VSI. And you know what that means?" He leaned forward to angrily smear out his cigarette, his left hand automatically reaching for the pack again. "That means DKA probably is going to have to eat that son of a bitch. Our coverage is good only during recovery, in transit, and in storage. Pissing around up on Twin Peaks at three in the morning isn't gonna be *no*body's idea of being in transit."

Ballard shook his head doggedly. He looked over at Giselle, said again, "Is Bart all right, or—"

"No. He's in a coma, they think he's got a skull fracture. He—"

Ballard stood up. "Which hospital?"

"You aren't going to do any good over there right now, Larry." Kearny looked up from lighting his cigarette. "Visiting hours don't start until eleven, you've got reports to type. I see you didn't get any in last night."

Ballard took a deep breath as if barely controlling himself, but said almost plaintively, "Dan, he *had* to have taken that car out for something besides a joy ride." Then, seeing the look on Kearny's face, he added hastily, "Yeah, yeah, I'll type the damned reports."

When Giselle left Kearny's office ten minutes later, Ballard followed her outside. Another batch of kids was capering and shouting in the fenced playground across the street, their cries as full of spring as geese V-ing north.

"How do you like that guy?" he demanded bitterly. "More worried about the damned Jag than he is about Bart."

"Twelve thousand bucks, Larry. And Bart *was* driving the car."

"I'm not so sure of that, either," said Ballard darkly.

She shrugged. Even in the current shoe styles she was only an inch or two shorter than his five-eleven-and-a-half. She had a short straight nose and a small mouth and blue eyes as clear as mountain water.

"There isn't any alternative, Larry. He was there, the car was there, and nobody else was."

"And both of 'em totaled? I'd like to hear what the Accident Investigation Bureau cops have to say." He started to turn away, but Giselle's voice stopped him. Her eyes were flashing, suddenly.

"Bart's not out at County General, you know, Larry," she snapped.

"Huh?"

"Of course Dan's worried about getting stuck for that Jag. But Bart's at Trinity Hospital in intensive care, a single-bed room with a private nurse as necessary. If you think all that's covered by the DKA health plan, you'd better hope you never get sick enough to test your theory."

"You mean that Kearny—"

"This morning, as soon as he got word. DKA's going to be picking up a lot of medical on this no matter *what* finally comes out about the Jaguar."

"Now you've made me feel like a bastard," said Ballard sheepishly.

"I sincerely hope so."

Three

Dr. Arnold Whitaker was mod. Bright red vest under a mustard sport jacket; psychedelic tie with a knot the size of a golf ball; the flowing sandy mustache of a World War II RAF pilot.

"No use going in to see him." He had a quick pattering voice, like mice in the attic. "Just a lump of black meat lying there in the bed at the moment. Poor pulse, respiration so bad we did a tracheotomy. Deep coma. Depressed fracture is my initial diagnosis; the skull x-rays ought to be up soon to confirm that. We've also done an EEG—"

"EEG?"

"Brain-wave study." He shot a cuff to check a watch gleaming with enough chrome to plate a bumper. "If there's nothing else . . ."

"I'd like to speak with Miss Jones." When the medico didn't react to her name, Ballard added, "Corinne Jones? His fiancée? She's supposed to be in there waiting beside his bed."

"Do you resent my letting her into the room and not you? I assume she's been sleeping with the man. I assume you haven't."

They were on the fourth floor of Trinity Hospital, a former old people's rest home which was in the process of being converted into a seventy-bed hospital.

Ballard, still hoping to get into the room, asked, "What are his chances of recovery, Doctor?"

Whitaker looked at his watch again, said "Damn!" explosively under his breath, said, "From which injuries?

The fractured skull, the cracked ribs, or the bruised knees?"

"Bruised knees?"

"From the dashboard. Common when the auto has gone over a cliff or embankment. Sometimes their feet are knocked right out of their shoes, leaving the shoes still tied."

"The fractured skull," Ballard said, then added as the thought struck him for the first time, "There isn't anything inconsistent with an auto crash, is there?"

"Um." Whitaker considered it, eyes agleam with interest. Finally he shook his head regretfully. "No. The fracture is on the side of the skull away from the driver's doorpost, but he probably received the injury when he was thrown from the car. He was damned lucky it didn't roll on him." Then he added cheerfully, almost to himself, "Of course, nothing in the injuries rules *out* the proverbial blunt instrument. But the *concept* is rather fanciful."

"He's a detective, Doctor. Detectives find out things."

"So do doctors—damned if I've ever figured out why." He looked at the monstrous skin-diver's watch again. "My wife gave me this, fantasies me as a scuba diver, I suppose. I imagine eventually we'll only be able to make it in a bathtub full of warm salt water. If you want an opinion to support a thesis, here: the nature of the injuries do not *preclude* felonious assault with something like a sockful of sand or a leather-covered lead blackjack."

"Thanks, Doctor," said Ballard. He added stubbornly, "I'd still like to see him, talk with Corinne."

Whitaker threw his arms wide in sudden resignation. "Oh, shit," he said precisely. The gray head of a nurse behind the desk snapped up to reveal a pair of shock-widened eyes. "Go on in. Your presence isn't going to make a damned bit of difference to the patient. You *can* keep your hands off the girl, can't you? She's very vulnerable at the moment."

Ballard almost got sore, grinned instead. "I'd *better* keep my hands off her. Bart's a former professional fighter."

"Former is probably right, Mr. Ballard. He might well end up with a plate in his head from this, residual weaknesses or even partial paralysis on the left side is a possibility—if he doesn't wake up a carrot." He then added, as an afterthought, "If he wakes up at all."

The nurse was staring at them again, reprovingly: a large fleshy woman with eyes right out of Buchenwald and a heavy bosom as comforting as a bag of cement. "Doctor, you have no right to say—"

"Shit," said Whitaker again, very distinctly. Her face went pale. He turned back to Ballard, said, "Seventy-two hours is as long as I would give him in coma without serious permanent brain damage either causing it or resulting from it. *I'd* have a hell of a hard time keeping my hands off Miss Corinne Jones in a darkened room—even if her boy friend was Joe Frazier."

He nodded and strode abruptly away toward the elevator. Ballard crossed the hall and pushed open the door of Heslip's room gingerly, half expecting to catch the nurse's beefy shoulder in the small of his back. He paused for a few moments, blinking, waiting for his eyes to adjust to the semi-darkness which contrasted so sharply with the bone-whiteness of the corridor. Only a single small night light was on; with the curtains drawn and the door reclosed behind him, it was really quite dark.

"Larry?" A dark figure rose from the chair on the far side of the bed. "Larry? Oh, thank God!"

He held Corinne for a moment as she clung to him with convulsive strength. The beautifully female body was warm in his arms. He released her quickly and stepped back, disturbed a little at his physical reaction to her. His eyes had accustomed themselves to the dimness enough for him to make out her features. She had a heart-shaped face so strikingly pretty that she approached true beauty.

"Rough, kid?"

"It's been so damned . . . *lonely*. Did you talk to the doctor?"

Ballard nodded. There was another chair, which he pulled up next to hers. But instead of sitting down, he moved to the head of the bed to stare down at Bart's still, grayish features under their absurd crown of bandage. Through his mind, like a sleep-learning tape under the pillow, reeled Bart's words from the night before: *I got something funny on one of the files. Probably just a coincidence, but I wanta ask what you think* . . .

"And?" prompted Corinne.

"No change in diagnosis yet," he said absently. It *couldn't* be that . . .

"What about . . . when he wakes up?"

"Russian roulette. *If* he ever . . ." He caught himself belatedly, pulled his eyes from Heslip's deathly still face to her. She was hunched over in her chair, crying silently. "Hey . . ."

He sat down beside her, but she shook off the arm he tried to put around her. Anger glinted through her tears. "I *hate* that bastard! Hate him!"

Ballard was confused. "Who?"

"Kearny. Him, and the goddamn detective business, and—"

"He's paying for the room," said Ballard. The tape had begun playing again. *Something funny . . . probably just a coincidence* . . . Something? No. Couldn't be. Nothing. Still . . .

"Big deal!" she exclaimed bitterly. "I've got a good job, I can manage Bart's hospital bills, don't need *his* charity. If it weren't for Kearny there wouldn't *be* any hospital bills. Wouldn't—"

"It could have happened against a ring post," said Ballard.

"He quit the ring almost four years ago . . ." She was crying openly by this time, without lowering her furious grief-stricken face or trying in any way to check the tears flowing down her cheeks.

"Only because he found something he liked as well."

"Oh, go to hell!" she exclaimed fiercely. Then she pressed her face against his shoulder and squeezed his hand so hard that his fingers reddened with trapped blood. "Oh, Larry, I'm so damned scared!"

The door opened to let a reedy red-headed nurse stick in a sympathetic face. "You'll have to wait in the hall."

They stood up. Corinne left her purse on the narrow rollaway table beside the bed. There for the long siege, Ballard thought. Better not tell her that seventy-two hours was the outside limit Whitaker was giving for Bart's unimpaired recovery. He held her hand as they went out; Whitaker was in the doorway. The dapper little doctor nodded.

"Couldn't keep your hands off after all," he beamed.

"What was *that* all about?" Corinne asked as they moved down the hall.

"He's got the hots for you," said Ballard. "He and his wife do it in the bathtub, and he's having a wish projection that you—"

"But it doesn't wash off!" she exclaimed.

It was the tag end of a joke among the three of them that, recalled, gave her momentary pleasure. Then her face tightened, got angry again. They had gone to the end of the hall to look down on drab, deserted Bush Street from a large round porthole-like unglassed window beside the rear stairwell. Corinne's emotions had always bubbled near the surface.

"At least in the ring the other guy's only trying to beat you, not kill you," she said.

"What do you mean?" demanded Ballard, more sharply than he had intended. It was too close to his own unformulated thoughts: *something funny on one of the files.* She was staring blindly down into the street, her face in profile severe of line like the Egyptian queen, Nefertiti, something like that—he'd seen her in an encyclopedia in high school, never had forgotten her.

Corinne met his eyes. "Bart wouldn't have been driving around in that Jaguar, Larry! What for? Cars don't mean anything to him, to any of you. You deal with them all the time."

"Don't tell me you think that somebody deliberately set him behind the wheel and then ran the Jag off Twin Peaks."

"Don't you?"

Ballard opened his mouth to say no, then closed it. Dammit, as she said, the only thing that made sense. He

straightened away from the porthole, suddenly in a hurry.
"I'd better, ah, get back to the office, kid. Giselle said
to tell you how sorry she is, and how much she hopes
that—"

"Kearny didn't send any kind words, did he?" Before
Ballard could speak, she added, "Don't bother to make
anything up so I'll feel good. The only thing that mean
son of a bitch could do to make *me* feel good is drop over
dead."

"Oh, hell, Corinne, make sense!"

"You're all the same, all of you!" she flared. "Giselle
included. Look at you! Can't wait around the hospital,
hell no. *You* have to get back to work . . ."

Start at the Taraval police station, get a look at the
patrolmen's report if he could, then up to Twin Peaks
—and why, if it *was* a phony accident, Twin Peaks, that
world-famous landmark which stuck right up from the
center of the city? Did that have any significance? And
after the accident site, down to the police garage under
the Hall of Justice to check if the Jaguar had automatic
transmission. Damned hard to work it with a straight
stick . . .

"If somebody *did* attack Bart," he said belatedly, "I
want to go after him."

"So even if you get him, what good would it do?" she
demanded bitterly.

"As much good as sitting here waiting for him to die."

When he was halfway down the hall, she caught up to
hold him again and kiss him on the side of the face and
wish him good hunting.

One hell of a girl, Corinne Jones.

Four

The black-and-white parked in front of DKA had ACCIDENT INVESTIGATION BUREAU lettered on the door, so Ballard went straight back to Kearny's office. It was blue with cigarette smoke and just barely big enough to hold, after he had come in, four people. Kearny looked up sharply.

"Where the hell have you been? I called the hospital—"

"I had a couple of cases to work," he said quickly.

"You want some coffee, Larry?"

He shook his head at Giselle. As he had expected, the cop was Waterreus, a huge Dutchman with a round red face and a big laugh and the eyes of a wild boar. He dropped in or called in often enough so Ballard was pretty sure he was taking DKA bread under the table for turning hot cars for them off their skip-list.

Waterreus nodded distantly, returned to the Xeroxed report resting on the upper of his crossed knees. ". . . three o'clock patrol found the Jaguar upside down on Twin Peaks Boulevard just about where Midcrest Way dead-ends." He looked up. "Midcrest doesn't actually come into the boulevard, it—"

"I know the place." Kearny knew most streets in the city.

"Okay. It hadn't been there when the patrol had gone through, oh, roughly an hour before. The injured man was a Negro male, head contusions, probably from doorpost, hell, I can skip all that crap . . . yeah. Here. Tracks down the side hill—which is maybe a hundred fifty yards high, maybe a forty-five-degree slope—these tracks indicate it went off on the next curve of the S, up above. Ah . . . subsequent examination showed it had not gone through the guardrail as first—"

"It *didn't* go through the guardrail?" Giselle asked, surprised.

Waterreus looked up. "What? Oh. No. That whole street, right from where it leaves Portola Drive, is guard-railed on the downhill side with that heavy steel freeway fencing, two and a half feet high, eight-by-eight uprights sunk in concrete. *Except* right there at the top, where the boulevard divides in half to make a double circle of the peaks. There's a little parking area on the right-hand side, and a little grassy knoll like, that comes down flush with the road. Maybe six, eight feet from where that guardrail starts."

It was Ballard's turn. He said, "I know the place."

"Must of been goosing her, coming back around the circle," said Waterreus, "and lost control. Hell, drunk like he was—"

"Bart wasn't drunk!" yapped Ballard, half rising.

Waterreus looked up from his accident report again. "Whole interior of the car still reeks of Scotch. The bottle busted when the car rolled."

"How are things at the hospital?" interrupted Giselle quickly.

"In a coma." Ballard's voice was grudging. "He was breathing so badly they did a tracheotomy. The doctor says if he doesn't wake up within seventy-two hours, he probably never will."

Waterreus stood up. "Tough luck about him—*and* about the Jag. You guys going to have to eat that loss?"

"Unless we can prove responsibility elsewhere," said Kearny.

"Pretty tough in a one-car, one-driver accident, ain't it?"

He shook hands around. Giselle followed him out of the cubbyhole bearing a tall narrow paper bag that clinked. Ballard slid down in his chair to cock one knee against the edge of the desk.

"How's that for superficial?" he sneered. "No mention of possible skid marks, no estimate of the speed the car was going when it went through that slot between the fence and the knoll, no mention of the automatic transmission, no mention of the fact that the head injury was on the side *away* from the doorpost—"

"Just what were those cases you checked out when you left the hospital?" asked Kearny mildly as Giselle came back in.

"I don't like that guy, he's always got his hand out," she said.

"Be glad he does." To Ballard, Kearny said, "You left your attaché case here with all of your case files in it. *All* of them."

"All right, so I was up on Twin Peaks to see where he went off," said Ballard irritably. "And I went down to the police impound garage at Fifth and Bryant to look at the Jag."

Kearny lit a cigarette. Waving out the match, he said to Giselle, "He thinks somebody drove Heslip up there with his skull already fractured, stuck him behind the wheel with the Jag pointed at that gap by the end of the fence, used Heslip's foot to jab down the accelerator with the car in neutral, then reached in the open window, flipped it into gear, and bailed out before it was going so fast it—"

"I didn't say that."

"But that's what you think." When Ballard was silent, Kearny thrust his massive jaw across the desk like Popeye sighting the spinach. "Isn't it?"

"All right, that's what I think. It's what Corinne thinks, too."

"There's some great facts to hand the insurance company."

"Whitaker says the injuries don't rule out a prior assault—"

"*Don't rule out. I think.*" Kearny smeared out the almost untouched cigarette, reached for another. "Facts!"

he barked explosively. "I'd *love* some facts. If somebody tried to kill him, I can tell the insurance company to pound salt."

"No skid marks," said Ballard. "No witnesses. Everybody knows that Bart is no boozer—"

"Everybody knows. Jesus, Larry, you've been with us for two years, you know what facts are."

"All right, goddammit, I don't have any facts!" Ballard began walking back and forth in front of the desk, slamming his open left hand with his fisted right, like a boxer warming up his taped fists against the target provided by the trainer's open palm. "Let me work Bart's assignments for a few days, I'll get you facts. This *has* to be in connection with something he was working . . ."

Kearny shook his head sadly. "Two years as a field investigator? I can't believe it."

"Without pay, then," said Ballard. "You want off the hook with the Jaguar. If I can furnish you with proof—"

Kearny's *"If"* dripped scorn. He drummed the desk with his fingers, glaring from Ballard to Giselle impartially. Finally he said, "What did that doctor say was the critical period? Seventy-two hours? You've got that to prove or disprove your idea. Have you checked Bart's case files?"

"Not yet. I didn't know—"

"Everything's on his desk. Type up a full list of your cases so Giselle can spread them around among the other men, then go through Bart's and narrow it down to possibles. I want a summary of those, and daily reports on all work done." He turned to Giselle. "Bart wasn't carrying anything except repossessions and chattel recoveries right now, was he?"

She narrowed her eyes for a moment. "No."

"Larry, eliminate cases on the possible list by finalizing them. Close them out. Got it?"

"Yes." In the doorway, Ballard paused. "Thanks, Dan."

Through the one-way glass they watched him cross the basement to Heslip's cubicle. Giselle cleared her throat. "It was good of you to go along with Larry so he could get it out of his system, Dan, but you were awfully rough on him. He *could* be right, you know. It isn't like Bart to—"

"He *is* right," said Kearny. He shook out cigarettes for them.

"What?" Giselle gaped as one hand groped behind her for the chair Ballard had vacated. She sat down without taking her eyes from Kearny. "You mean that all the time—"

"Larry's involved, emotional on this. I had to get him thinking like a cop again." He mimicked Ballard's voice. *"I think.* Jesus!"

Giselle feathered smoke through her nose, felt a quick stir of anticipation. This was it, one of those rare moments for which she stayed on at DKA despite her M.A. in history and the offer of a teaching fellowship from S.F. State. The hunt. It got into your guts, twisted them; and Kearny was the best hunter there was. She waggled her fingers at him.

"Give," she said. "Tell me what I missed. What Larry missed."

Kearny put his elbows solidly on the desk. "All right, the call came in at three-thirty, at home. Operating assumptions: Bart Heslip wouldn't joy-ride a repo; if he did, he wouldn't be drunk; if he was drunk, he still wouldn't smash it up."

"But just assumptions," said Giselle quickly. "No facts."

"No? I talked with the driver and the steward in the Park Emergency Hospital over by Kezar Stadium, and they gave me what you and Larry just heard Waterreus say: the booze in the Jaguar was Scotch."

"Ri-i-ght," said Giselle, chagrined. "And Bart never, not ever, drank anything but bourbon. When he drank anything at all."

"That made me go up to Twin Peaks to look it over at five o'clock this morning." His gray eyes gleamed in the rough granite face. "The only place a car could go over, he went. The *only place,* you follow me? So then I came down to the office. And Bart's car was parked across the street where it still is." He paused. "Unlocked."

Giselle sat up straight, suddenly. "Bart would never—"

"Exactly. Ballard missed that, too. And something else he missed. Look at this."

He opened his desk drawer, flopped a trifolded sheet of paper on the desk. Pink report carbons were stapled face-out to the back of it. Harold J. Willets. Scrawled across the front was Heslip's notation, *Repo,* with the date beneath it.

"Lying alongside the curb outside the front door," said Kearny.

"He could have dropped it, not noticed . . ."

He shook his head to the question in her voice. "No way. What do *all* our men do when they call in a repo? They write down the cop's name and shield number. Here it is, see? Delaney, 7-5-8."

"What time did Delaney log in Bart's call?"

"One-oh-one A.M. I talked with Delaney; he said they joked back and forth, Bart sounded perfectly sober then. Ballard got here at one-twenty-five. That means that in a little over twenty minutes, Bart had to take off in a repo—to buy a quart of Scotch, let's say—in such a hurry that he left his own car unlocked, and left the office locked but didn't bother to set the alarms."

Giselle shook her head. "That just doesn't make it, Dan."

"Now it gets cute. What was he going to do until Larry got here?"

"Type reports."

"Sixteen of them, remember. That's what he told Larry on the radio. We both know he always writes his notes on the face of the last report carbon stapled to the assignment sheet. We also know that he keeps those case sheets which are ready for reports over his car visor. He had the Willets assignment sheet with him because he'd just phoned it in to the cops, you follow me? But—"

"But he would need the others from over the visor," said Giselle in excitement, "and he would go out to get them . . ." She ran down. "But how do we know he was carrying the Willets assignment in his hand when he went out?"

"Because I found it in the gutter. Right where he would

drop it if he got sapped as he came out the door. If he *hadn't* been carrying it, it would still be on his desk with the condition report. Or it would be missing."

"Missing?"

"The rest of them are missing."

Giselle's eyes went wide with shock. "All of his case assignments are missing?"

"No, not all. I *think* all of those he worked yesterday —the ones that would have been over the visor. We know he picked up three cars last night, right? Well, *no* assignment sheets were over the visor ready for reports, none of those three repo assignments were in his briefcase. And none of those that *were* in the briefcase have notations of work done yesterday. Yet he told Larry he worked sixteen of them."

"So I'd better go through all of the open files, type a list of the ones Bart was carrying, compare that with the list of case assignment sheets Larry finds in Bart's folders—"

"Right," said Kearny. "Another thing Larry missed. He spent twenty minutes with that doctor, never asked him whether there was alcohol in Bart's bloodstream. I asked when I called over there; all the Scotch was down the front of his shirt."

"If we remind the police of that—"

Kearny shook his head. "The cops have it as an accident, let them keep it that way for a while. *Somebody* tried to knock off one of my men, Giselle. Somebody panicked on *some* case after talking with Bart sometime yesterday, and acted damned fast to take him out. Then he grabbed all of those case assignments to mask which one he was really after—actually, of course, he was after Bart's notes on the back of it. He couldn't know that our routine is so standardized we'd realize the assignment sheets were missing. So then he locked up after running the Jag out, forgot to lock Bart's car door, didn't know about the burglar alarms. Strictly a panic operation all the way, but he almost got away with it. Almost. We're going to find that bastard, and—"

Ballard burst into the cubicle, almost stuttering with

excitement. "Dan! Giselle! Every single damned one of Bart's case sheets that he worked yesterday is missing! That means—"

"All except this one," said Giselle dryly.

He grabbed it out of her hand. "Yeah! Dirt, grease, oil on it . . ." He looked at Kearny. "In the gutter out in front?"

Kearny nodded.

"Then he *did* get it here. Went out to cross the street to his car for the other assignments, and—"

"You had seventy-two hours as of two o'clock this morning to convince me," said Kearny. "Twelve of them are already gone."

Five

Sixty-eight. That was how many cases Giselle and Ballard, working together, finally were able to confirm as being carried by Heslip at the time the Jaguar had gone off Twin Peaks.

Current: active files on which work would have to be done. There were thirty-seven of them, ranging from two months old to those assigned to Heslip the day before, and which still needed their twenty-four-hour first report.

Hold: eleven of them. Open cases, still active and still in the area, but cases on which the clients had advised DKA that the subjects were in the process of working out arrangements with them.

Skip: fourteen skips. When the subject had left the area covered by the field agent—literally, "skipped out" —he became the responsibility of the inside skip-tracers (usually girls) who worked the files by phone. The field agent held these files in abeyance until new leads had been developed.

Contingent: Heslip had been carrying only seven contingent files. The DKA fee (setup, time-and-mileage, and skip-tracing charges) was paid on contingent cases *only* when—and if—the case was successfully closed. These were worked only sporadically by the field agents and skip-tracers.

Of these sixty-eight files, they had been unable to find assignment sheets in Heslip's briefcase for fifteen. With the Willets case included, that tallied with what Heslip had said on the radio the night before—which was maybe the only hopeful thing in the whole setup. Because it could be a damned obscure motive connected with any of those sixteen cases.

At eight o'clock, after an indigestible sandwich at a coffee shop, Ballard leaned back in his chair and groaned. His coat had been discarded long ago, and his tie. He could smell himself. Man, for a shower and ten hours of sleep! But eighteen of his seventy-two hours were gone, and he hadn't even been out of the office yet. Hadn't called the hospital again, either.

He dialed, got the reception desk, and was switched up to the floor desk. Whitaker was gone for the night, so he asked if Miss Corinne Jones was in Heslip's room.

"I'm sorry, sir. I can't leave the desk."

It was ten paces from the desk to the door of Bart's room. Ten paces. What the hell had ever happened to Florence Nightingale?

"Could you tell me the condition of the patient in room three-eight-two?"

That she could do. After a pause, the depersonalized voice came back on. "The patient is still in coma, sir."

Just beautiful. Dark and silent in there, all systems shut down. Not Bart. The systems *had* to start up again, the quick smile had to light the dark features, the teeth gleam, the muscular boxer's hand slap the thigh, the voice laugh, "You an' me, baby, we cool!"

Find the son of a bitch. At least you can do that much. Before Kearny takes you off the search; only fifty-four hours left. Can't let that happen. So, have to be cold and steady. Here for one thing, to find the son of a bitch. No, not even that. To find the subject. That was it, find the subject, eliminate those cases one by one, coldly, efficiently, until only one was left.

And that would be the right one.

Ten o'clock, sixteen had been reduced to six. On eight of them, the reports had indicated there just was none of the passion or hatred or fear one associates with attempted murder. And thirty minutes before, at 9:30, Kearny had dropped in on his way home and had promptly eliminated two of the eight Ballard was then considering.

"Forget the three we *know* were repo'd last night. No subject is going to come down here and beat Heslip over the head, grab his assignment sheets—and then leave his own car here."

"Bart said on the radio that Willets had given him a hard time because he was black."

Kearny nodded thoughtfully. "He might have come after Bart, not to get his car back, but because he wanted to whup a nigger?"

"Yeah."

"Why take the assignment sheets without taking his own?"

"He could have just not seen it in the gutter. Hell, *I* didn't—and I wasn't scared and excited like whoever slugged Bart probably was."

"If anybody did," said Kearny flatly. "Okay, leave Willets in as a possible until you can check his movements last night."

Which left six.

Of course he still could be wrong, Ballard knew. He might have missed or misread something in the files, it might really be *none* of these. But at least he had a starting point. And Giselle and Kearny would be coming through the files behind him to check his conclusions. Which reminded him to type up the list of "possibles" and leave it on Kearney's desk.

1. Harold J. Willets, 1972 Mercury Montego. Residence address, 736 Seventh Avenue, San Francisco. Age, 44; 3 dependents; white.

Ballard regarded this a moment, then added *Reason Why Included:* SUBJECT HATES BLACKS.

2. Joyce Leonard Tiger, 1972 Cadillac Coupe de Ville. Last known address, 1600 Fell Street, San Francisco. Age, 28; single; white. *Reason Why Included:* SUBJECT PROBABLY IS A WHORE.

3. Charles M. Griffin, 1972 Ford Thunderbird. Last known address, 3877 Castro Valley Blvd., Castro Valley.

Age, 41; single; white. *Reason Why Included:* SUBJECT
MAY BE AN EMBEZZLER.

4. Fred Chambers, 1971 Buick Skylark. Residence ad-
dress, unknown. Work address, The Freaks Bar, Clement
and Tenth Avenue, San Francisco. Age, 22; single; white.
Reason Why Included: UNIT WAS REPOSSESSED IN BA-
KERSFIELD BY CLIENT TWO MONTHS AGO. SUBJECT STOLE
IT BACK AFTER CLIPPING CLIENT'S MAN WITH A TIRE
IRON.

5. Timothy Ryan, 1956 Chevrolet Sedan. Residence
address, 11 Justin Drive, San Francisco. Age, 21; married;
white. *Reason Why Included:* SUBJECT THREATENED
CLIENT'S REPRESENTATIVE WITH A MACHETE WHEN RE-
COVERY OF UNIT WAS ATTEMPTED.

6. Kenneth Hemovich, 1970 Plymouth Roadrunner.
Residence Address, 191 Stillings Avenue, San Francisco.
Age, 19; single; white. *Reason Why Included:* SUBJECT
LIVING WITH 32-YEAR-OLD WOMAN WHO IS TRYING TO GET
HER THREE KIDS FROM THE HUSBAND.

There they were, the six of them. Was the attempted
murderer among them? He *had* to be. There wasn't
enough time to find him if he wasn't one of these six. In
each case there was a history of or a motive for violence.
A black-hater. A whore whose pimp would be oriented
toward violence as a problem-solver. An embezzler;
tracked down for his car, he would also go to jail. A rock-
group leader at a hip bar who had stolen the car back
once, had attacked a man to do so. A young man with
an old car (hence, probably rodding it up, hence, probably
a car-lover) who had threatened violence to retain his
vehicle. And a nineteen-year-old kid living with an older
married woman—an always explosive situation, especially
with small children involved.

Before leaving, Ballard typed up duplicate assignment
sheets for himself on each case, and stapled to the back
of them the spare gold-colored copy of all reports and
memos in each file. Before leaving, also, he set up his
swing.

New men with DKA usually would start with one file
and work every address in it until they found something.

It was the way it was done in detective stories. But experience soon taught them to arrange their field work by address. Thus, the swing: a loop or circle through the city or that portion of it where there were addresses to work. Since Ballard was trying to discover why Heslip had gotten a busted head, he was trying to retrace Heslip's probable movements the day before. Which meant reworking all leads, no matter how basic. This rearranged the cases by addresses:

1. Joyce Leonard Tiger—1600 Fell Street.
2. Harold J. Willets—736 Seventh Avenue.
3. Fred Chambers—The Freaks, Clement at Tenth Avenue.

That took care of the Western Addition and the Richmond District. After that he would cross Golden Gate Park and head out through the Sunset District, south toward the San Mateo County line. Doing that would add:

4. Kenneth Hemovich—191 Stillings Avenue.
5. Timothy Ryan—11 Justin Drive.

Very often, of course, you were led off on tangents by something hot you learned at one of the addresses. But at least you started out with a game plan. His, tonight, left him with one case on which he could do nothing until the next day.

6. Charles M. Griffin—3877 Castro Valley Blvd., Castro Valley.

The trouble was that the possible embezzler lived in the East Bay. Heslip had merely been assigned to check out Griffin's San Francisco work address, which was a parking garage down on First Street. Which, of course, would be closed for the night by this time. Tomorrow for Mr. Griffin.

Six

Joyce Leonard Tiger.

The Fell Street address was just beyond Central, on the other side of the Park Panhandle from the decayed Haight-Ashbury where the love-children syndrome had ended in muggings, murders, bad trips, and addiction. No 1972 Cadillac Coupe de Ville with the subject's license number in the area, a black neighborhood even though the subject was listed as being white.

Sitting in the car, Ballard read over the single report —Heslip had gotten the case only two days before.

Per Mrs. Shirley Jackson, landlady at 1600 Fell Street, the subject had skipped out the previous Wednesday owing nearly four hundred dollars in back rent. Real name: Joyce Leonard. But she had been living common-law with a black named Tiger. Mrs. Jackson didn't know if Tiger was a first, last, middle, nick, or assumed name. Tiger would leave in the early evening with the subject, then the subject would come back alone with a man, and keep coming back alone with a steady stream of men who stayed between fifteen minutes and an hour each. When the stream stopped, Tiger would return.

The Mary Magdalene lay, as old-time field agents like O'Bannon would call it.

Heslip also had checked with the subject's listed work address, Bethlehem Steel's Accounts Receivable office at Third and Illinois. Subject terminated "for cause" (unspecified) on 12/15 of last year. Merry Christmas.

The only other given information (facts listed on the

case sheet when it came to the field man) was that she had a mother named Thelma Barnes in Stockton.

Ballard checked the names above the mailboxes in the gaudy vestibule of the cheap new building. No Leonard. No Tiger. His watch said 10:42. He rang the *Mgr* bell.

Mrs. Shirley Jackson was a bride or her husband had been at sea for a long time. She sat on the arm of his chair during the entire interview, squirming slightly under his explicit sexual caresses. All three of them—she, her husband, and her husband's hands—seemed totally indifferent to Ballard's presence.

"Like I told the other gentleman from your company, she just up and moved out in the afternoon. When she knew I wouldn't be here."

"Cadillac, huh?" said Mr. Jackson suddenly. He was a lean sad-faced black man whose long skinny fingers roamed his wife's body like electricity. "That woman went through more cars—like to went through a car a week, something on that order. I remember two Fords, two Mercurys, then she had a Dodge. Now a Cadillac."

"I had to help her up the stairs last month," said the wife. She was small and round and cute and shiny as black patent leather, with remarkably dainty feet and hands and a roll of flesh under her breasts that was irresistible to those busy hands. "She'd been in a fight with Tiger, lost two front teeth."

"Did the men stop coming after that?" asked Ballard.

"Only for a day or two."

"Even without them teeth she was a fine-looking woman." Jackson's hands pinched. "Yassuh, *fine*-looking woman. Few bumps and bruises don't . . ." He ran down, then volunteered suddenly, "Sheeit, she was always pretty beat-up-looking anyway. Her an' Tiger used to bust up each other an' the furniture till they'd pass out, most nights."

"Anyone see her move out?" asked Ballard, writing on the gold carbon of Heslip's report.

"The Blodgetts," said Jackson promptly. "Folks in 3-A. Said it was a big red moving van, too big for the little bit of furniture they had wasn't broke. Black driver 'bout Mack-truck size, according to Miz Blodgett."

"You didn't say nothing about that to me," said Mrs. Jackson. Her tone of voice gave the busy fingers pause.

"I disremembered, honey."

"If I thought you and that Mrs. Blodgett—"

"Could that have been San Francisco Van and Moving?" asked Ballard. They were just across Stanyan from Park Emergency where Bart had first been taken, he knew, which put them in the neighborhood. And they had red trucks.

"Hey, could be at that," beamed Mr. Jackson, who seemed to welcome the interruption.

The case sheet, folded in thirds, went above Ballard's visor. S.F. Van was a good lead for the next day, but Joyce Leonard Tiger was dead for tonight.

Harold J. Willets.

Ballard parked at the curb by the Safeway on Seventh Avenue. Behind him, on the corner of Fulton, light spilled from the big Chevron Station, but Seventh itself was totally still and quite dark. Eleven o'clock on a week night in the Avenues was always dead.

Harold J. Willets, boy racist. The last case Heslip had worked before he had gotten it.

Nice if this would be it, end it right here. Of course, he couldn't be sure unless Willets broke down and confessed or something, but on the other hand, a man who has beaten someone over the head is liable to exhibit nervousness under questioning, especially if head-beating isn't his normal profession. Willets' was driving a bread truck.

Even so, Ballard sat in the car for a few moments with a sort of empty feeling in his stomach. But it was the routine which saved you. You did what you always did. And hell, he was just over twenty-five, weighed 184, took a size-forty-four jacket. A good left end in high school, handball now on free evenings, abalone-diving up the coast on weekends. Able to take care of himself physically.

But then he would have said the same thing and more

about Bart Heslip—until last night. He grunted, and got out of the car.

It was anticlimactic. Willets wasn't home.

But lights were on next door, and five minutes of conversation there just about took care of Harold Willets. He'd spent two hours at their house the night before, 12:15 to 2:15, telling about the black son of a bitch who'd come and taken his car. The neighbors had told him they couldn't do that, and today Harry had gone to see an attorney.

"They can do that," said Ballard flatly.

"How do you know?"

"I'm one of they."

Which left only five possibles on his list.

Fred Chambers.

Heslip's reports showed that the subject could be found six nights a week at The Freaks, playing in a hot rock band called Assault and Battery. Was he kidding? Awfully damned appropriate for a cat who had slugged the client's man down in Bakersfield and then had boosted the Buick right out of the bank storage lot after it had been repo'd.

On three different nights Heslip had tailed the subject from The Freaks. Once Chambers had taken a cab, twice had ridden with friends, to three different addresses which subsequent investigation had shown were not his own. Heslip had not spoken to him, since the client's orders were explicit: *Repossess on sight. Do not attempt personal contact.*

He could be it, all right. See Bart recover the Buick, follow him, attack him, then take back the Buick and the case sheets to disguise the fact that the car had been repo'd in the first place. Think Bart was dead; try to make manslaughter look like an accident.

Ballard drove out Balboa to Tenth Avenue, then cut over to Clement. He turned right, went by The Freaks and on down to Ninth, over to Geary, up to Eleventh, past Clement to California, back down to Ninth, over to Clement, back up to Tenth. The classic search pattern, usually carried in reports as *cruised the area, could not spot unit.*

Only this time, when coming back up Clement, he saw a white 1971 Buick Skylark in the white zone in front of The Jolly Coachmen, directly across from The Freaks. It hadn't been there five minutes earlier. License, 331 KLZ. Jackpot. Fred Chambers' car.

Ballard parked around the corner on Tenth. His hands felt cold as he folded and pocketed the assignment sheet, got out the sixty-four GM master keys, window picks, hot wire. Ready to go. So go.

Ballard walked up to the Buick and began running the keys on the door. Key 14 turned slightly, stuck. He worked it. It popped over. He jumped in, slammed and locked the door. Dammit, dammit! Key 14 just would not work the ignition. He began running the set.

A short, stacked, very pretty brunette in hip-hugger purple cords and a funky tie-dyed silk blouse came from The Freaks, looked at the Buick casually, did a double-take, then ran across the street toward him. Ballard kept running the keys.

"What are you doing in there? Get out of that car!"

Ballard shook his head, kept running the keys. She turned and ran back across the street and into The Freaks, her solid rear jouncing pleasantly in the purple cords.

Up to key 27 without success. Hell.

Twenty-five or thirty patrons, mostly men, burst from The Freaks in a clot. Ballard, still running keys, could identify the subject from Heslip's reports: blond hair down over the shoulders like Prince Valiant, a Jesus Christ mustache and beard. Not Christlike, however. When the door wouldn't open, he began beating almost hysterically on the window with a clenched fist, kicking, shouting, "Get out of there, you fascist son of a bitch. I'll off you, pig bastard . . ."

The black-haired girl cried, "Fred! Fred! Here's the keys!"

The subject tried to unlock the door. Ballard held down the lock knob with one hand, ran keys with the other. The girl had a second set; the subject went around to the other side. Ballard slid into the middle of the car, held down a lock knob with each hand. It was getting hairy. A heavy-set lumberjack-type wearing slacks, no shoes, no shirt, and a paisley vest that left bare his hairy meaty arms, began pounding on the windshield with the heel of his hand, trying to bust it in.

The girl disappeared; Ballard immediately used that hand to run keys again. Number 53, still no joy. Over his shoulder he saw that the girl had stopped a cruising black-and-white, was gesturing and pointing and crying. You don't know it, honey, but thanks.

One of the cops advanced on the Buick with his holster flap unbuckled. He rapped on the window with a gloved knuckle, stuck a tough cop's face against the glass. "Okay, buddy, out of there. Easy!" he called.

Ballard picked up his repossession order from the seat and held it against the window. The cop studied it, turned abruptly to the girl. "Hell, lady, he's a private cop. He's legal."

"But he can't just—"

"He's got the paper that says he can, lady."

The subject, while Ballard had been showing the repo order, had finally gotten his door unlocked. He jumped in beside Ballard. "Out, pig bastard, or I'll break you apart!"

Ballard met his eyes. This he could handle. "Sorry, Mr. Chambers. I have to take the car."

Chambers began cursing shrilly. Behind the beard his face was contorted; spittle flecked his mustache. He still made no actual move to touch Ballard, however. The girl had unlocked the other door. The cop opened it to stick his head in. "Any chance of waiting until tomorrow on this?"

"No known residence, five hundred bucks delinquent, he stole the car back from the client's lot in Bakersfield after it had been repossessed down there, is currently out on bail under an aggravated assault charge in connection with that. You tell me, Officer."

"Yeah." The cop turned back to the girl. "That's it, lady. He wants it now."

"I . . . all right." She caved in abruptly, leaned across Ballard to tell the subject, "Give him the keys, Fred."

"I'll give him shit!" Fred yelped. "I'll—"

Just then the lumberjack went for the partially open door. The cop moved casually to block him, but the beefy youth shouldered him roughly aside.

The second patrolman, a huge black who had been leaning against the squad car with his arms folded, the picture of noninvolvement, lunged forward like a fencer. His giant black hand plucked the attacker like an orange. "That's a *cop* you're shoving, daddy-o," he crooned. He had a dreamy, hopeful look on his face. The lumberjack's hands curled into fists; the cop said softly, "Yeah!"

He slammed the other man up against the squad car in the classic spread-eagle as if he were made of papier-mâché. As he frisked the youth and plonked him in the back seat of the squad car, the crowd quieted magically. The black cop called him in to the Hall of Justice for a make on possible wants, reading his statistics from his driver's license.

The girl, meanwhile, had started crying. "Fred, give him the keys!"

"I'll give him something, I'll—"

"Like you gave it to the black boy last night?"

"I . . . what?"

"One of our men," said Ballard. "He's in a coma. If he happened to catch up with this car last night like I did tonight—"

"Oh, no," said the girl in a sick voice. "You can't . . . Fred wouldn't . . ."

"Like hell Fred wouldn't," said Ballard.

"Look, I've been driving the car ever since Fred started his gig here," she said desperately.

"What time does his last set end?"

Chambers said, in a small voice, "One-thirty, one-forty-five. Man, I didn't clobber any spa—any black. I *didn't,* man."

The cop looked pointedly at his watch. Chambers slid hastily out; the girl dropped the keys in Ballard's lap as if suddenly glad to be rid of them. When Ballard pulled away he could see, by the rear-view mirror, that the lumberjack was being released from the prowl car— which meant he was clean downtown.

Halfway to the office, Ballard suddenly started shaking. He had to pull over to the curb and park for a while. It had been a pretty close thing back there. The Freaks' clientele seemed trying to live up to the name.

But as he started up again and headed for the office, he drew a mental line through *Chambers, Fred.*

Seven

A heavy hand on an auto horn jerked Ballard's head up. His eyes were bloodshot; he had drooled on the desk top. Man, dead asleep. What time? He looked blearily at his watch. One-twenty. A shiver ran through him as he got upright, yawned, knuckled his eyes, pulled on his topcoat. Yeah, yeah, I'm coming, for Christ sake.

Twenty-four hours ago, here at DKA, Heslip had been getting it. How was he? Any change? Hell, too late to call. Ballard stumbled past the Chambers Buick, set the alarms before pulling the door shut behind him. Involuntarily he looked right and left before crossing the sidewalk to the Yellow Cab he'd called. Nobody, of course.

"Yeah, make it Geary at Tenth Avenue."

He settled back in the rear seat, to fall asleep immediately. The cab stopping woke him up, he paid the driver, got his receipt, walked down Tenth to his company Ford. Shivering, he got the motor started, tried to knuckle sleep from his eyes. Then he grinned to himself. Maybe he ought to go around the corner for a beer at The Freaks. Yeah, sure. What he ought to do was go home, get some sleep.

But only forty-eight hours left to Kearny's deadline. And two more cases lined out for tonight yet.

Kenneth Hemovich, 191 Stillings Avenue.

Where the hell was—oh yeah. Out off Monterey Boulevard somewhere. He checked the map, then used Park

Presidio to get through Golden Gate Park to Nineteenth Avenue in the Sunset. Patrick Michael O'Bannon, the best field man DKA had next to Kearny himself, had played as a kid in the sand dunes where the Sunset District now was. He said. You could never tell, with O'B. He was a blarney Irishman for sure.

Ballard turned up Congo from Monterey, was immediately into a maze of streets which curved and climbed up the flank of Mount Davidson. The air coming through the rolled-down window to keep him awake was wet and heavy. Stillings was only two blocks long; he parked a block from 191 to recheck the file.

Heslip had started the Kenneth Hemovich case with a given work address of 1680 16th Street. This turned out to be a private home where nobody had ever heard of the subject. Cute. The given residence address had been 644 Mount Vernon Avenue. Not much better: a black woman with eight children and a TV addiction. She hadn't removed her eyes from the twenty-six-inch color screen, Heslip's report stated, during the entire interview.

At least she knew the subject, had even seen him three times with Virginia Pressler, the thirty-two-year-old girl friend. The Mount Vernon woman had cared for the three Pressler children (eleven, nine, and eight) until three weeks before, when old man Pressler had come and abruptly taken them away.

Hemovich and Virginia Pressler were living together as man and wife "in the sight of man but not before the Lord God Almighty," she told Heslip. She didn't know *where* they were living together. Written neatly across the face of this gold report carbon, in Giselle's hand, was the address where Ballard now was: 191 Stillings Avenue. Ballard's blood quickened. Had she gotten it verbally from Heslip? Had Bart been here last night to learn . . . *what?*

Ballard went up the street, his shadow dancing long and thin before him. The under-the-house garage was locked, but he could see through the mail slot that a car was in there. His flashlight could give him the color, blue, but not the make. The file carried no color for the Hemo-vich Roadrunner.

When he stepped back out on the sidewalk, a voice called from the totally dark doorway of the house. "Hey, what the hell you think you're doing?"

"Looking for Ken," Ballard said promptly.

"Hemovich? You a friend of his?"

Something in the voice tensed his gut muscles. Choose right, you might crack the case. Wrong, you blew the whole file. The gut muscles had to serve for intuition. "Hell no. I want to repossess his car."

After a moment the porch light went on. Ballard went up to the door. The voice said, "I figured that son of a bitch would get into trouble with somebody 'sides me pretty soon. Ran off with my wife . . ." Which explained where Giselle had gotten the address: from the *Polk Directory*.

"Wouldn't know where they're living, would you, Mr. Pressler?"

The door opened wider, on a sour-faced man dressed in robe and slippers, spike-haired from sleeping. His eyes gleamed briefly, but he shook his head. "Ginny works down at Kearny and California, big *in*surance company. Homestead."

"How about Hemovich?"

"Sheet-metal work when he's working. He ain't work-ing often."

"You wouldn't remember the color of that Roadrun-ner, would you?"

"Wouldn't I? Yeller. Yeller as a damned canary."

It was chilly; Ballard could see their respective breaths in the porch light.

Pressler suddenly chuckled. "When I heard you at the garage door, thought it was him, tryna get at the kids again. Ginny wants 'em so bad she can taste it—the bitch." His face closed up like a fist; he brought a double-barreled shotgun out from behind the door frame. "He comes around next time, I'm gonna blow his head off. Right off. A burglar, y'see?"

Ballard saw. And hauled his ass out of there.

Timothy Ryan, 11 Justin Drive.

Nothing had been done on this assignment by Heslip —unless it had been done the night before. Given information: the subject was twenty-one years old, white, just married, had quit his job at Southern Pacific Railroad yard, so no work address was known. The client was a two-bit Mission District auto and accessory dealer who specialized in old cars for conversion to dune buggies, drag cars, rods, and the like. He had sold the subject the 1956 Chevrolet, then had financed racing flats, chrome rims and lugs, a chromed engine head, and virtually all the vehicular ornamentation known to man to bring it to a total contract price of $1,989.81.

The subject had paid for three months, then had quit. Perhaps when he had gotten married?

Justin Drive was in a small, cozy residential area on the fringes of Bernal Heights. No lights were on in the house, the '56 Chevy was nowhere around, and he was too tired to care whether he woke people up or not.

"I'm not going to open this door!" warned a quavery female voice.

"Unless Tim Ryan's there, I wouldn't want you to."

"We're the Greers."

"Don't know the Ryans?"

"No, we've just been here a week, we . . . what?" She turned from the door; her voice timbre and intonation were definitely Negro. No Ryans here. Her voice came back, ". . . husband says Mr. Ryan moved in with his father-in-law. A Mr. Harrington. Out on some street comes in right where San Jose and Ocean come together . . ."

Back out Mission toward Daly City, south through a night-emptied city. Phone booth . . . whoops. A total of 123 Harringtons with residential addresses. Back to the car for the city map. Streets where San Jose and Ocean intersected . . . Yeah. Geneva, Seneca, Oneida, Delano, Meda, Otsego. Back to the phone book. There it was.

Patrick Z. Harrington, 61 Oneida Street.

They were old single-residence dwellings, mostly stucco, mostly set back from the street behind narrow lawns.

Concrete drives led to under-the-house garages. A standard construction of the 1920s and '30s, the houses rubbing shoulders as did most houses in San Francisco; it was a city of long, narrow building lots.

The garage door was shut but not locked; it went up with only a subdued spronging of well-oiled hinges. Four-year-old Chrysler Imperial, black and dusty. He noted the license number out of habit. Raw data collected as you came into a case often broke it later on.

The door opened immediately when he touched the bell, despite the TV squawking softly in the background. Hell. Dead end again. A stooped middle-aged black man peered at him from the doorway.

"Late for socializing, son," he said softly.

Ballard tried to put apology into his voice. "I must have been given the wrong address, I wanted a Harrington who has a son-in-law—"

"I'm a Harrington, son. Patrick Z. No son-in-law, though."

Hell again. He couldn't help asking it anyway. "What's the Z stand for?"

"Zebediah."

That figured. He rubbed his jaw to keep from grinning. Wait until he gave O'Bannon the needle about *this* one. Harrington. Ryan. "Do you *know* a Tim Ryan?"

"Stepson. My wife's boy by her fust husband, they's a difference between son-in-law and stepson. He ain't even married. Tim's off to work now, works at an all-night gas station down on Geneva Avenue somewheres. Don't rightly know which one, a Union, I think." He leaned forward to peer at Ballard critically. "This about that car of his?"

Again, instant decision. Again, let the gut reaction decide. You didn't last in this business very long without developing a feel for the cases you were on. "That's it. Big John's Used Cars had to hire an independent detective agency because your boy ran their man off with a machete . . ."

"Hell, son, know what that feller said? Right to Tim's

face? Said, 'Ain't no broke coon gonna default on no car payments to us.' Now, I ask you."

Ballard grinned and shook his head. It figured. Everything else the client had given them had been wrong, why not that, too? He'd probably find the 1956 Chevy was actually a 1908 Stanley Steamer with a smokestack or some damned thing.

"You go drive up and down Geneva," said Harrington. "Can't be too many stations open all night. Tim don't want what he ain't paid for."

Ballard thanked him, turned away, then stopped and turned back. "Can I ask you a question, Mr. Harrington?"

"Fire away, son. If you hit something tender I'll holler."

"How come Harrington? Ryan? I thought I was looking for a bunch of Micks."

The old man slapped his knee in sudden glee. "Hell, son, I thought you'd never ask! We're *black* Irish, cain't you tell?"

It was a Richfield station three blocks north of Geneva on Old Bayshore. What the hell, it was one of those cases. At least Tim Ryan, a stocky, wide-shouldered black kid with an incongruous stub nose, was far from belligerent.

"When he said that to me, Mr. Ballard, I just . . . well, I just lost control, I guess. I sent in a payment yesterday, I can send another tomorrow . . ."

Sure as hell, Tim Ryan hadn't hit Heslip on the head. He'd have to check further, and his assumption was subject to what Dan and Giselle thought, but the kid just wasn't right for it. And he had a money-order stub for the payment, too . . .

"You'll have to cover our charges," Ballard said. "And for God sake keep the thing current from now on." He got back into the Ford, asked casually through the rolled-down window, "Another agent from our company wasn't around to talk to you on this yesterday, was he?"

"You're the only one I've seen." Ryan's sudden grin resembled his stepfather's even though there was no blood relationship. "Only one I *want* to see!"

And so to bed, after stopping by the office to write notes on the cases he had worked, so Kearny would know what was going on until he had a chance to write regular reports. To bed, to sleep, perchance to dream—he'd played Macbeth in a high school play. To dream, like hell. Dead to the world before he hit the pillow.

Eight

"Larry's working himself out of a job fast," said Giselle Marc. She, O'Bannon, and Kearny were in the tiny cluttered middle clerical office at DKA, where the big radio transmitter for contacting the field units was located. On the wall behind her desk was a huge map of the city.

"I read his notes," said Kearny. He was waiting for the water to boil in the little kitchen alcove in one corner of the room. "He'll want to check with The Freaks before totally eliminating Chambers, but we can scratch Willets. I never liked him for it anyway. And it looks like Ryan is out of it."

"The black Irishman?" laughed Giselle.

"I fail to see anything funny in that," said O'Bannon with great dignity.

Patrick Michael O'Bannon was forty-three, with freckles and flaming red hair and a drinker's leathery face. He had started as a collector for a retail jewelry firm, had switched into investigations, had come with Kearny from Walter's Auto Detectives at the founding of DKA. Right now he was sitting on the edge of the desk that held the radio, swinging one leg. A voice blared, he pushed the Transmit button on the stand-up mike.

"No, SF-8, that isn't funny, either." He released the button so he was not transmitting. "This new guy, Dan, this SF-8, where did you get him from? I didn't know it was Hire the Mentally Handicapped Week around here."

"I like the pimp for it, myself," said Kearny, loftily ignoring O'B. They had just finished their weekly fight about O'Bannon's expense account, and Kearny had lost —as usual.

"Tiger?" asked Giselle.

"I put out a feeler with our police informant on him and Joyce Leonard. If she *is* playing for pay, the Vice Squad might have a current res add on her."

"What about the embezzler?"

"From Castro Valley?" Kearny shook his heavy graying head. "The guy's a dead skip, Giselle—not one damned live address in the file. Bart just had the one work address to check on a reconfirm."

"How is Bart this morning?" O'Bannon's lean features looked drawn, as if it had been a rough night. For O'B, it usually was.

"No change," said Giselle. "Still in a coma."

The intercom buzzed, she picked up, said "Yeah?" and listened. She held the phone out to Kearny. "Waterreus the BB-eyed Dutchman."

Kearny listened, spoke, listened, nodded, said "Thanks" and hung up. "Joyce Leonard was picked up for soliciting last January, her driver's licence has been revoked for drunk driving, and they've got a warrant out on her for overdue parking tags. Waterreus said he'll check the location she's been drawing the tags and call back." To O'Bannon he said, "Try to raise Ballard, O'B."

"KDM 366 calling SF-6. Come in, Larry."

"He won't be on the street yet, Dan," objected Giselle. "It's only a little after nine, his note said he was going home at four this morning."

"He'll be working. That deadline I gave him is only forty-two hours off."

Larry Ballard was working, all right, feeling a hell of a lot better for four hours' sleep, a shower, a shave, and breakfast in a greasy spoon on Ninth Avenue near his Lincoln Way apartment. But he was not in his car to answer O'B's call. He was in San Francisco Van and Storage at 791 Stanyan Street, waiting for a black mover named Chicago. Chicago, he had learned, would have moved Joyce Leonard if anyone at S.F. Van and Storage had.

Ballard was also waiting for Chicago because everyone else at S.F. Van—every single person—was drunk. Every living soul, at 9:38 on a weekday morning. Leaning against the L-shaped counter and looking through the inner door to the storage warehouse, he could see them, passing the bottle around. Apparently most of them slept there at least part of the time; several cots were set up.

A blocky round-faced man who had said he was Bonnetti, office manager, weaved his way to the door. He gripped the frame with blunt calloused fingers. He regarded Ballard owlishly. "Oojusangon," he said. He blinked deliberately and solemnly and tried again. "Oo . . . you. You jus' ang . . . *h*ang on. Good ol' Chi-town'll be in pr'y soon. 'Kay?"

"Okay."

" 'M gonna shraiten out 'morrow. 'Kay?"

"Okay."

Ballard waited for the crash as he turned away, but Bonnetti, office manager, was made of the stuff of heroes. He didn't fall down.

The front door opened and a black man as black as Bart Heslip, which was very black indeed, came through at an angle so he wouldn't take out the door frame with his shoulders. Ballard raised his gaze from the second button on the man's blue coveralls—which was the button level with his eyes—to the massive tight-clipped head. The features made the late Sonny Liston seem like just another pretty face.

"Chicago?"

"The Windy City flash himself." Chicago's voice had the resonance of a hi-fi woofer with the gain all the way up. He looked past Ballard to the back room. "Those bastards all drunk again?"

"Still."

"There's that, ain't there?" Chicago said pensively.

"I'm surprised any of them still have their chauffeurs' licenses."

"Most of 'em don't. But you want anything moved, old

Chi-town will give you his *personal* service. Safe as houses, silent as the fog, gentle as a kitten, Chicago will—"

"I'm trying to find a white whore named Joyce Leonard who's shacking with a black pimp named Tiger."

"Whoo-ee!" yelped Chicago, startled. Then he started to roar with laughter. "Sheeit, mother, you shoulda been a preacher! You *do* call 'em as you see 'em!"

"Am I wrong?"

"Hell no, she tried to sell me a piece in the new apartment when I got her moved in. Last Wednesday, it was." He shook his head. "White meat don't turn me on, I got Maybelle and four cute kids to home. Wouldn't shoot that Joyce with your artillery, man."

"You remembered her pretty quick," said Ballard.

Chicago laughed again. "You're a cop or something, ain't you? Like private or something?" He nodded in approval. "I remember 'cause ain't every day I get offered white meat, not even off'n a turkey like her. Likewise, a little black feller was in asking the same questions, was, let's see—"

"Day before last?" said Ballard eagerly.

"That's it. Little feller, wouldn't go a hundred sixty pounds, but *moved*. I mean, like a dancer."

"Bart Heslip," said Ballard almost fiercely to himself.

"Good friend, huh?" said Chicago. "In big trouble?"

"Big as it can get without being dead."

"Tiger, maybe? I know that cat, *mean* mother. They at 545 O'Farrell, apartment . . . hell, can't remember. On the second floor."

Chicago wouldn't even take a couple of bucks for a beer. A hell of a man, Ballard thought as he switched on his radio. As soon as it quit whining he unclipped the mike and depressed the red Transmit button. "SF-6 calling KDM 366."

"Go ahead, Larry," said Giselle's voice.

"I've got a new res add on Joyce Leonard, en route there now—5-4-5 O'Farrell. I think they might be it, Giselle. Bart was at the moving company two days ago."

Kearny's voice came on. "KDM 366 to SF-6. Forget

Leonard and Tiger, Ballard. Repeat, scratch Leonard and Tiger, over."

"But they're *right* for it, Dan. Over."

"SF-2 is picking up the Cadillac right now from a parking lot in the three-hundred block of Eddy."

SF-2 was O'Bannon. He didn't mind O'B picking up the car even though it was his case now, but dammit, why was Kearny so sure that Tiger was not the one who had slugged Bart?

"Where did the location on the Cadillac come from, over?"

"A police informant was running down the subject's parking tags, and found that Tiger and the subject were involved in a fight in a Tenderloin bar at ten o'clock the night before last. Over."

"10-4," said Ballard. He understood, all right. Arrested at ten on the night Bart had gotten it, they wouldn't even have been out on the street by one o'clock, let alone hitting anyone on the head.

"Tiger is in jail, the subject is in the hospital. He went for her with a razor, took out one of her eyes with it. 10-4?"

"10-4," repeated Ballard. He reclipped the mike on the dash, said aloud, "Son of a bitch, anyway."

Leonard and Tiger had looked so *damned* good for it.

Charles M. Griffin.

The JRS Garage, 150 First Street, was at first glance just a square open door in the side of a building across from the East Bay Bus Terminal. But when Ballard drove across the sidewalk and under a red sign offering parking at *35 cents per ½ hr,* a huge shadowy parking garage stretched ahead for a half a block. What a place to bury a car you were trying to hide! Maybe that's what Griffin had done with his.

He drove up the narrow aisle between the parked cars until he was waved down by a round-faced black man in red coveralls with JRS and JOE stitched above the respective breast pockets.

"I'm not leaving it—just want to talk with one of the bosses."

"There's three partners," said Joe. He was a large-bodied man with tight-clipped, tight-curled hair and an infectious grin. Ballard found himself grinning back. "Park in that middle stall between the two pillars. Leave the keys in case I have to move it."

The office was a concrete box set beside the cross-piece of the H-shaped aisles. Behind the open counter a sandy-haired man named EARL, who looked like an ex-Navy chief, was clearing the cash register with the single-minded ferocity of a commuter-train conductor punching tickets.

Ballard checked his assignment sheet. "Is . . . um . . . Leo Busilloni or Danny Walker or . . . um . . . Rod Elkin around?"

"Leo's out checking lots, Danny's up at the Bush Street garage, and Rod's out getting a sandwich. If you want to wait, you can go right through to the office."

Ballard went by Earl and across the small room to a slightly larger room beyond. Pasted to the front of the bottled water dispenser was a typed notice: DUE TO IN-CREASED TAXATION, RISING PRICES, INFLATION, AND HIGH-ER WAGES, THIS WATER IS NOW TWICE AS FREE AS IT USED TO BE. The inner office had windows all around to chest-level which looked out into the garage, three wooden desks, and some straight-backed chairs just inside the door.

Ballard moved a copy of *San Francisco Screw* off a chair to sit down. *Screw*'s front page had a photo of a young couple proving that the underground newspaper was aptly named. Ballard, who would rather do it than look at it, passed up the paper for the bulky Griffin file, glad of having a few extra minutes to review it.

DKA Oakland originally had gotten it as a straight collection on February 21, when the subject was delinquent 1/17 and 2/17 in the amount of $108.64 each on a 1972 T-Bird. Contract balance had been $5,542.31 at that time, and these were the fourth and fifth payments respectively. All of the earlier payments had been at least a week late, one of them seventeen days. DKA Oakland immediately had run into a stone wall, because the subject had left his residence address of 3877 Castro Valley Boulevard, Castro Valley, a full month before he had given it to the bank as his res add when buying the car.

The case had immediately been reassigned to the SF office as a *Repo on Sight* from the work address.

The subject was gone from his job, also.

The March 17 payment was not received, making it a deadline deal on which the client's ninety-day recourse would expire in one month. That meant the client would have to eat the car if recovered after April 17, so all the stops had been pulled: the file went to skip-tracing, the car went on the company hot-sheet for state-wide distribution, East Bay and SF police checks were made for warrants or parking tags, the state DMV was checked for the address to which his license tabs and most recent driver's license renewal had been sent. Credit-checking services were utilized, his insurance broker contacted, the dealer and salesman who had sold him the car, his lawyer, friends, neighbors, his only living relative (an aunt), by phone and in person.

Nothing. Absolutely nothing. Dead end. Blank wall. Charles M. Griffin was a dead skip.

On April 19 DKA charges were billed to date and paid by the client, and the case was put on Contingent status. On May 8, after a routine file review, the case was assigned to Heslip for a single purpose: to recheck with the ex-employers whether they had mailed out the subject's W-2 at the end of January, whether it had been returned, and to what address it had been mailed.

That had been on Monday. On Tuesday, with no report on the case in the file, Bart had been whapped on the head. Earlier, that afternoon, he had said to Giselle casually that "the cat from the East Bay is gonna turn out to be an embezzler." Bringing Larry Ballard to JRS Garage on Thursday.

"You wanted to see me?"

"Oh. Yes." He stood up, stuck out his hand. "Larry Ballard with Daniel Kearny Associates."

"Rod Elkin." They shook.

Elkin was a tall, lanky, good-looking man with sharp features and a big nose. He had abundant black curly hair and sideburns, and a wry quizzical expression that looked habitual. He wore corduroy slacks and a wide leather belt.

"Daniel Kearny Associates . . ." He was frowning. "Wasn't one of your men in here the other day?"

"Tuesday?" asked Ballard quickly.

"I didn't talk with him. Leo did." He flopped into the ancient swivel behind his desk and cocked a lean leg over the edge in what was obviously a favorite position.

Ballard sat down again. "You don't know what they talked about, do you?"

Elkin frowned. "Something about Griff's W-2?" He nodded to himself. "That's it. Wanted to know if we sent one out. We did."

"Did it come back?"

"Not that I ever saw. But—"

"Sure as hell did," snapped another voice from the doorway.

A bulky bald man in a white parking-attendant's coat came through the doorway to stare at Ballard accusingly. The phone rang. Elkin made a wry face, said "JRS, Rod," and started listening. He waved a hand at the bulky aggressive man, said to Ballard, "Leo Busilloni, he's the one talked with your man," transferred the phone from his left hand, and began writing things down on the back of an envelope.

"You from that same private-eye agency as the black guy?" demanded Busilloni aggressively. He talked, moved, reacted in the quick staccatos of a man in good condition, a younger man than his bald crown suggested. He sat down at a desk stacked high with computer print-outs.

"Yes. Did you show the W-2 to our other man?"

"He got all excited. New address from what you had in the files," said Busilloni. Ballard started to get excited, also. The bald man opened a drawer in his desk, rummaged. After about thirty seconds he said "Shit!" explosively. "Never can find a damned . . . it was a Concord address, I know . . ." He looked up. "He must have moved there last fall, after his mother died. The P.O. forwarded the W-2 to Concord from Castro Valley, then it was sent back here. First we knew he'd moved."

"You don't remember the street?" asked Ballard tightly.

"California Street." Busilloni squeezed his eyes shut for a moment, opened them. "Yeah. The house number was 1830." The bald man hustled out again, after adding that Elkin had gotten stuck with Griffin's job. Griffin had been the man who counted the cash.

"A license to steal," said Elkin, hanging up the phone. "You guys are after that T-Bird?" Ballard said they were, and Elkin shook his head. "Why do the middle-aged swingers, when they start swinging, always get a T-Bird? He had a VW before his ma died."

"What about this idea that our other field agent got about Griffin cooking the books?"

"The hell of it is, *I* just don't know. What does your man say about it?"

"He's not saying anything. He went off Twin Peaks in a repossessed vehicle the night before last."

Elkin stood up abruptly. "I want to show you something."

They went down a short corridor to a closed solid metal door. It was unlocked. Inside was a battered swivel chair and a table made longer by an old door laid over it. There were no windows, just a ventilating fan. On the door was an adding machine, a stack of cloth bank money bags, some untidy piles of receipts, and a squat gray-metal machine with a round shiny maw on top, set at an angle like a giant phone dial. This had a metal basket with a spout. Along the bottom of the machine were five chrome drawers.

"Coin-counter," said Elkin. "Sorts 'em into the drawers by size—halves, quarters, dimes, nickels, pennies. Also keeps a running total which you can crank off whenever you want."

"This is where Griffin worked?"

"Yeah. All alone. Locked himself in." He leaned against the table and folded his arms. "His job was counting the receipts. Cash. He made the pickups from the garages each morning, checked the registers against the pickups, counted the self-park coin boxes, totaled credit-card sales, made up change for each station's daily operations, and got the money ready for the armored car to deliver to the bank."

Ballard nodded. "So nobody knew exactly how much money you were taking in except Griffin, right?"

"Right. The month's receipts *never* balance—hell, it's a physical impossibility. If we're within a hundred bucks of register receipts at the end of the month, we think we're doing great. Depending on how long he was stealing—if he was—we could be twenty, thirty thousand bucks down the tubes. I only took over three months ago, after Griff took off. I've got it so screwed up we're lucky to make payroll each week."

So there it was, Ballard thought as he slid beneath the wheel of the Ford ten minutes later. Elkin had given him a lot more background, a description of sorts. Griffin's mother had died a year before; in the fall of last year Griffin had suddenly gone on a diet, lost thirty pounds, bought new clothes, moved out of the big old house in Castro Valley, let his balding hair grow long and raised a crop of big puffy muttonchop sideburns. When he had bought the T-Bird, Elkin had asked him about all of the blossoming-out in his life.

"He said that his mother's will was out of probate, he'd come into some money," said Elkin. "He was our bookkeeper for five years, steadiest employee we had—then his ma died. When he took off, he called in sick two days in a row, last time on a Friday. On Monday, no call. He never showed up again."

Griffin *could* be it. If twenty, thirty thousand bucks *were* missing, that sure as hell was a motive sufficiently heavy for murder. The hell of it was, nobody at JRS Garages was going to be able to confirm or deny shortages until an audit was made. And none would be made until the end of the fiscal year after June 30. None of which was going to help Ballard with a deadline which was now just thirty-eight hours away.

But maybe he had another way to go. Listed in the file was the phone number of Andrew W. Murson, who was supposed to be Griffin's lawyer.

Nine

What he *wanted* to do was buzz over to East Bay and check out the new res add on Charles Griffin, but there still was Kenneth Hemovich and his Plymouth Roadrunner, and reports to type on the work done so far, and a condition report on the Chambers Buick, and a number of phone calls. Since the Homestead Insurance Corporation was only a few blocks the other side of Market from 150 First Street, he went there first.

Parking was always a bitch in the financial district; he finally put it in a garage off Halleck Alley and walked over. Homestead Insurance had three floors. He called from a lobby phone booth. "Do you have a Mrs. Virginia Pressler employed there?"

"Yes, sir, I'll ring—"

"I don't want to talk with her," he said quickly. "Just give me Personnel." A pause, a new feminine voice on the line. "Yes, ma'am, this is John Daniels with Bank of America. We're verifying employment on a Mrs. Virginia Pressler."

Pause yet again. "Mrs. Pressler has been with us since June, 1968. Commercial underwriting department—"

"I see. Now, we have found that her residence address of 191 Stillings Avenue is no longer current. Since she is applying for a rather sizable loan, we would like to confirm her new residence address for our files . . ."

"Just a moment, sir."

Ballard grinned to himself. Smooth as silk, they were going to give him the address where Virginia and Hemovich were shacking. Run out there tonight, drop a rock on that Roadrunner . . .

Click. Another new voice. "Mrs. Pressler speaking."

Goddamn that personnel girl! Quick, who was carrying the insurance on the car? Continental, that was it. "Ah . . . Mrs. Pressler, this is Mr. James Beam from Continental Casualty. We have a notation here that you are currently driving a 1970 Plymouth Roadrunner, yellow in color, California license F-A-Z 8-0-6, registered to a Kenneth Hemovich . . ."

"I'm . . . sure there must be some mistake." Nice sexy voice for a chick of thirty-two—bright chick, stalling for time, trying to make Ballard out. "Did you say Hemovich?"

"Kenneth. We have been carrying the insurance on the vehicle, and since you are driving it—"

"You couldn't possibly know . . ."

"There's never any answer at Mr. Hemovich's home phone, and our mail is being returned." I hope the bastard *has* a phone. No listing, but of course there wouldn't be.

"What address did you send the mail to?"

Sharp chick! Slide by that one fast. "We have to notify him of cancellation of his auto insurance, and—"

"Cancellation?"

"Working for an insurance company yourself, Mrs. Pressler, you know how costly it is to be put into Assigned Risk—"

"I see." That one had gotten to her. "Can I try to reach Mr. Hemovich and have him call you a little later, Mr. Beam?"

"Any time between one-thirty and two-thirty, the number is 431-2163." To psych her from going through the Continental switchboard, which would blow it, of course, he added in a snide voice, "Your *switch*board gave me *three* wrong extensions before I got through to you."

The phone number, 431-2163, was one of two unlisteds that DKA kept exclusively for incoming calls on cases where it was essential that the caller didn't know whom he was calling. Virginia Pressler probably would now get together with Hemovich on her lunch hour, and have him make the call when she could be coaching from the background.

"I really want to thank you for that Stillings Avenue address."

Giselle Marc looked up from her desk. "I thought that the husband might . . ." Then she belatedly caught the sarcasm in Ballard's voice. "What was the matter with it? Nobody there?"

"It's just lucky that I don't look nineteen any more. Old man Pressler was waiting around with a twelve-gauge shotgun for Kenny-baby to show up."

"And you were checking the garage?" She made a face. "Pâté-de-foie Ballard. Did you stop by to gripe, or was there something?"

"Two—no, three questions."

"Go."

"Where are 342 phone prefix numbers located?"

"San Mateo County. Two?"

"I'm expecting a call for Beam on 2163. Will you switch it to Dan at the same time you give it to me? I'll clue him in ahead."

"Will do. Three?"

"Has anybody been out to the hospital to see how Bart is doing?"

"I was by last night, called this morning. No change—except that Corinne has lost about ten pounds." She looked around almost furtively. "What does she have against Dan, Larry?"

Ballard sat on the edge of her desk. In the background, the radio was blaring something about burned-out distributor points. He shrugged. "She just hates the detective business."

"So what else is new? So do all the agents' wives."

"Yeah. But their husbands aren't lying in a hospital with a fractured skull the way her man is."

Giselle nodded. "Sometimes I wish . . ." She let it die. "Anyway, he's still in a coma." Her voice got suddenly vicious. "Get the bastard, Larry."

First he had to find out who the bastard was. Griffin? Hemovich? Which reminded him to stop at Kearny's office to brief him on the expected phone call. Then into his own cubicle for phone calls and reports. Phone first, of course, so the latest info could be incorporated into the reports.

The manager of The Freaks was a man named Tunulli, who wasn't there, but the bartender gave Ballard the home phone. Tunulli readily confirmed that Fred Chambers had been on the stage at The Freaks in full view of a hundred people until 1:35 A.M. on Tuesday night. Cross off Chambers, definitely.

From the cross-directory, Ballard got the number of the Union gas station on Old Bayshore, caught the lessee there. Yeah, Tim Ryan worked the night shift for him five nights a week, Monday through Friday. Hell yes, he was there Tuesday night. From ten o'clock until six Wednesday morning. Swear to it in *court?* C'mon, buddy, you gotta be . . . Just a minute. Got an idea. Could he call Ballard back?

He could. Meanwhile, Ballard dialed 342-4343, the San Mateo number listed in the file for Andrew W. Murson, attorney-at-law, who was supposed to be Charles Griffin's lawyer. Mr. Murson was just going out the door on his way to court, said the secretary. Could he . . . *Very* urgent?

"Andrew Murson here."

"Yes, sir, I'm trying to reach one of your clients, a Mr. Charles M. Griffin, on a very important matter. Do you have any idea where—"

"None at all," cut in Murson dryly. "I represent Mr. Griffin in a very limited capacity; I was his mother's attorney, and after her death last year I probated her estate. Charles is principal heir under the will, which is the only connection I have with him. If this is an overdue bill, I would suggest you not bother me with—"

"Attempted murder," said Ballard in his nastiest voice.

"Attempt . . . whoa! On him or by him?"

"By, if he's involved at all."

Murson waited a long moment, then sighed. "It's on

Castro Valley Boulevard in Castro Valley, I can't recall the number. It's in the book."

The given address, of course; no good on a dead skip like Griffin. Ballard hadn't expected anything else. But the exchange had softened Murson up for the information Ballard did want. "Ah . . . you said you handled the mother's will. Is that out of probate yet?"

"In California? These things take time."

While the lawyers leached out what they could, Ballard thought. He thanked Murson, hung up, stared blankly at his stack of report forms. Exactly, Mr. Murson. Will not yet out of probate. And where did that leave the inheritance that Griffin had claimed to JRS Garage was his source for the new car, new clothes, all the rest of it? Unless the old lady had been coffee-canning cash for him that hadn't shown up in the estate; and Ballard doubted that.

Which might or might not mean, of course, that Griffin was the attacker. One thing was sure: if he was, as of Tuesday night (Wednesday morning, really) he had still been in San Francisco. Which gave them a hot rather than a cold trail to follow, which in turn meant he wasn't going to remain a dead skip for much longer. But could Ballard find him before Kearny's deadline, now only thirty-six hours away?

The phone rang.

Switch gears. And files. Virginia Pressler and Kenny Hemovich.

But it wasn't. It was the manager of the Union gas station calling back on Tim Ryan.

"I thought I remembered my kid saying that he was down there until after two, putting new plugs and points in his car, and turning the brake drums. Tuesday night, it was. It was slow after midnight, and Tim was helping him. Hell of a mechanic, that Tim . . ."

Two of his original six possibles left. Kenneth Hemovich. And Charles M. Griffin. One or the other. Or neither? Dammit, *had* to be one of them. Or else he was right back to Wednesday morning, trying to convince Kearny that Bart actually had been attacked.

The phone again. This time it was Hemovich. Ballard heard the click of Kearny picking up just behind him. Hemovich *sounded* nineteen on the phone: halting, unsure, his voice tending to slide into a higher register as he talked. In the background, Virginia Pressler, coaching. What the hell did a woman with three kids, one of them eleven, want with a nineteen-year-old punk for a lover?

Vitality. Virility. Old man Pressler hadn't looked like much of a sexual giant. Or just the kid's youth, maybe?

"Ah . . . I understand from, ah, Mrs. Pressler that you claim my, ah, insurance is being canceled."

"That's right." He took a flier. "The bank tells us they can't get in touch with you, they claim their contract is out of trust and that they are about to declare it null and void. Under the circumstances . . ."

Whispers. Then he said, with Virginia's voice almost audible behind him, "You mean the *bank* is asking you to cancel my insurance?"

"That's right." Dammit, she *was* smart.

"Tell them to go ahead. I'll place other coverage elsewhere."

Kearny's heavy voice suddenly came on, rich and oily and insinuating. "Mr. Hemovich? Joe Bush here, of California Citizens legal department. I just happen to be here in the Continental office discussing this case with Mr. Beam at this moment. *You* know, and *I* know, Mr. Hemovich, that the contract is being voided for only one reason: nonpayment of the auto notes under the contract agreement. We don't even know who's *driving* the car—"

"Mrs. Virginia Pressler." No coaching; they'd covered that beforehand.

"A *third party?* Mr. Hemovich, you're *way* out of trust on this contract!" Kearny was winging it, without even the file in front of him and with just the sketchiest briefing. There just wasn't anybody better around, anywhere. "First, we need Mrs. Pressler's home address—"

"I can't . . . give you that." Furious whispers. "I mean, I don't *know* where she lives."

"You gave the car to someone you don't even know?"

"Yes. Ah . . . no. Ah . . . I mean, I never see her . . .

Ah, I never drive it, she has it, she, ah . . . yes, she just moved . . ."

"Then we'll need *your* current address."

Again, consultation. "I . . . can't give you that, either. I—"

"You don't know where *you* live?"

"No! Ah . . . I've got, ah, personal problems . . ."

An irate husband with a shotgun, for openers. Kearny was saying, ". . . don't understand your attitude, Mr. Hemovich. I'm afraid I'm going to have to advise the bank to go for Grand Theft, Auto, on this one—"

"Hey! Wow, ah, listen, I . . . Look, I'll *pay. I'll pay!* And I'm working, honest. I—"

"I haven't found you honest yet, Mr. Hemovich," he said coldly.

"I *am* working. Valencia Shee—"

The phone was slammed down abruptly. By Virginia, of course. Kenny and Ballard still had an open line even though the outside connection had been broken, and Kearny said, "I bet she's giving him hell right now. Not that he told us anything useful . . ."

Ballard was already into the Yellow Pages. Since he hadn't turned in his reports yet, Kearny didn't know what old man Pressler had told him the night before.

"Here it is, Dan. Valencia Sheet Metal Company, thirty-two-hundred block of Mission." He looked at his watch. "He'll be there until four-thirty, he won't expect us because they don't know I found out he works in sheet metal. I'll go out as soon as I finish these reports."

Ten

Valencia Sheet Metal Works was on Mission just south of the angled Valencia Street intersection. An old building in an old neighborhood which had witnessed successive streams of Micks, Wops, Portagees, Spics, and Spades; each group, in the fullness of time, moving out and up and being magically transformed into Irishmen, Italians, Portuguese, and Spanish-Americans. The blacks, mainly, were still there; but they were beginning to eye with disdain the illiterate Hong Kong Slants. Thus they passed, one after the other, in that curious upward mobility which seems to characterize American ethnic groups.

Ballard, who was not even subconsciously aware of any racial debts, was concerned only with spotting the yellow Roadrunner and avoiding the punk in the dune buggy who ran the red from Valencia Street.

No Roadrunner, of course. Virginia Pressler would be driving that. Hemovich, if he had wheels at all, would be herding some heap of tin that had slid out of the bottom end of the Blue Book years before.

Valencia Sheet Metal Works was a big monolithic-pour concrete building with dirt-opaqued, thickly wired windows, and huge loading doors wide and high enough to admit interstate semis. Inside, screeching saws bit through metal; galvanized steel dust lay over everything; weird truncated modern sculptures which were actually made-to-order duct-work crowded the shop area.

"*Who?*" shrieked the little Chicano Ballard had picked as not possibly being anyone named Hemovich.

"Ken!" Ballard bellowed. "Kenny Hemovich—"

"Oh. Heem. *Ken.*" He pointed across the cavernous room to a lathe beside which a skinny kid wearing a Giants cap and new leather gloves was lethargically stacking sheets of galvanized steel. "On the duct-work tin."

Ballard mouthed thanks made silent by the shrieking saws, then went up the wooden office stairs as soon as the Spanish-American turned away. At the head of the stairs was a tiny, cramped, but blessedly soundproofed office with a wooden counter behind which two harassed-looking females labored. One was young and blond and typing on an old manual, the other was older and doing bookwork.

" 'Nye help you?"

"I need Kenny Hemovich's home address," said Ballard. When the ledger woman made a movement toward the intercom page system, he added quickly, "He's out on one of the trucks, I checked. I'm taking over the payments on that yellow Roadrunner of his, and he wants me to pick it up tonight, before the bank repossesses it or something. Only all I've got is the old address."

"We just got the new one ourselves," said the blond girl.

She gave Ballard an unexpectedly brilliant smile; when she bent over to get the personnel folder from the bottom drawer of a file cabinet, he watched with a quick faint stirring of lust as her miniskirt rode up almost to her buttocks. Glancing away, he caught the ledger woman watching him watching, and winked at her. Also unexpectedly, she bent her gray head over her bookwork and started to giggle. The curve of cheek he could see turned bright crimson.

The blonde came back to the counter. "Here it is," she said happily. "5-0-7 Nevada Street. I'll write it out for you."

When she handed him the slip of scratch paper, her fingers rested on the back of his hand. Again, that brilliant smile. Maybe she hadn't been so unaware of the miniskirt after all. Ballard went away. Ledger was still giggling.

Before getting back under the wheel, he removed his sport jacket. Hot afternoon for May; the Mission District got more sunshine than most other areas of the city. Maybe he should have asked the blonde for her phone number. He bet the shopmen all hung around the bottom of the steep open stairs when she went up to the office each morning, if she always wore skirts that short. He got the radio going.

"SF-6 calling KDM 366 Control." When Giselle's voice told him to go ahead, he said, "I've got a res add on Hemovich. 5-0-7 Nevada Street, San Francisco. I'm going over there now to check it out. After that I'll try to beat the rush hour across the Bay. Over."

"10-4. We'll inform Oakland Control that you'll be in their area this afternoon, over."

"Ashcan that. They always try to rope me in on one of their lousy repos. Last time I got two ice-picked tires out of it."

In a very la-di-da accent, Giselle said, "A-ten, a-four, a-Roger, a-Wilco and out. Your Majesty."

Ballard clipped his mike, grinning, and started out Mission toward Cortland Avenue, which gave easiest access to Nevada. That Giselle.

The 500 block was a steeply slanted street sliding over an arm of Bernal Heights toward the incredible maze of overpasses and underpasses, ramps and cloverleafs which marked the confluence of the Interstate 80 and Interstate 280 traffic streams. Houses crowded down the hill waist-to-shoulder, all of them needing paint, all of them with garages on the ground floor, short steep drives, and tiny slanted squares of lawn just big enough to blow your nose on.

The Pressler-Hemovich shack-up was apparently still too tender for the permanence of house purchase contracts; 507 was a stucco bungalow that looked like a rental property. If old man Pressler didn't blow Kenny-baby's head off, Virginia probably would get sick of mindless all-night humping and adolescent pimples, and eventually go home to papa and the kids.

The garage was locked but empty. Ballard checked the mailbox, saw a window envelope from the San Francisco Department of Social Services addressed to Hemovich.

His lip curled unconsciously. Nineteen years old, on welfare. At least Virginia had gotten him off his dead butt and back to work. A woman, like a dope habit, was expensive to support. Even a working woman.

Ballard opened the trunk of his car, found a piece of thin copper wire, looked about and saw no window shades or drapes or curtains flapping. He clipped a short piece of wire and stuck it in the lock of the garage door. He drove off grinning. Poetic justice, that—although he didn't believe that Hemovich had clouted Bart over the head. Not after seeing the kid in person. The attack on Bart had required a deadly decisiveness that Hemovich just didn't have.

Of course, maybe Virginia Pressler did. She was smart, obviously strong-minded. Could she also be murderous?

To hell with them. Nothing to be done about them until tonight anyway. Which left Griffin, and the East Bay. But down on the freeway the cars were already clotting up even though it wasn't yet four o'clock.

Why not wait until after six, use the time to drive out to Trinity and see Bart? He hadn't been there since his first visit yesterday morning. *Yesterday?* God, it seemed like a week since he'd stared down at that dark, still face on the pillow, with Corinne sobbing in the background.

He pulled the car over and stopped beside a sidewalk pay phone near a small neighborhood shopping area. He sat in the car for a few moments. The hell of it was that he didn't want to visit the hospital, either. Didn't want to see Bart just lying there.

He *had* to pull out of it. But according to Whitaker, every hour that he stayed in the coma meant . . .

Had to get the mother that did it. *Had* to. If he hadn't connected by the end of the seventy-two hours, and Kearny cut him off, he'd have to quit his job and keep looking. There was no other way to go.

He got out of the car, got the phone number from the telephone book, asked to have Whitaker paged. The girl on the switchboard said he had already left the hospital. She switched Ballard to the third floor, this time to a nice-sounding nurse who *had* heard of Florence Nightingale.

"No, gee, I'm terribly sorry to have to say he's still in coma, no change at all in his condition."

"His, ah . . . Miss Jones wouldn't be around, would she?"

"I'm sure she's in his room. That poor girl has barely been out of this place since . . . just a sec. I'll send an aide to get her."

When Corinne's voice came on the phone it was flat and exhausted, limp as a home permanent in the rain. Trying to compensate, Ballard put as much spurious warmth as he could into his own. "Hi, kid! This is Larry—"

"I know who it is. Why haven't you been around to see Bart?"

A lump of black meat lying on the bed . . . How do you give that as a reason to the girl who loves him? "Well, ah, Corinne, I've, ah . . . they said at the office that there'd been no change . . ."

"Don't you even *care* enough to come see him?"

"It isn't that, kid. You see, I—"

"Or do you feel that he's all done anyway, so what the hell's the difference?"

"You know that isn't it, kid. It's just . . . well, I've only got about one more day to find out who did it—"

"Who cares?" she asked in a bone-weary tone.

"I care, I . . . Look, Corinne, you need sleep, food— the nurse tells me you've barely been out of the hospital since he was brought in. When was the last time you ate a meal?"

She sighed. "I don't know. This morning sometime. Last night. *I* don't know, what difference does it make?" She suddenly burst out, "Oh, Larry, he just *lies* there! Why can't they *do* something?"

"I guess Bart has to do it himself, from what Whitaker said. He *will* do it, Corinne. He's never backed down from a fight yet."

"Please come over here, Larry." Her voice held an almost wistful note through the fatigue. "I need you. *Bart* needs you."

Ballard looked at his watch. "All right, kid, I'll try to

make it. I'm way out in the Mission right now, I can't *guarantee* anything, but——"

"Thanks, a lot, sport," she said flatly.

He cursed, once, hung up the already dead phone. Back in the Ford, he dug out his maps for Southern Alameda and Contra Costa Counties. Shit, he just couldn't hack it there at the hospital. And he couldn't really take the time, anyway. Only about thirty-four hours left to his deadline.

Then he thought, guiltily: How many hours does Bart have left?

Eleven

The Mysterious East Bay, as Herb Caen always called it in his daily *Chronicle* column. Ha. About as mysterious as a bag of dirty laundry. A big hot sprawl of nothing, like L.A., with all those cute names the subdividers loved. Glorietta. Saranap. Gregory Gardens. Housewives driving around in shorts and hair curlers, men drinking beer at the drags on Sunday.

Christ, he was tired. Used up.

And the clock pushing him, pushing all the time, so he couldn't afford any mistakes, couldn't miss any nuances. He didn't have time for backtracking. He had to get everything there was to get out of a single interview; rechecking leads burned up precious minutes, hours.

One nice thing about Castro Valley, however: he was far enough south to be out of radio reach of Oakland Control. Half a mile away Interstate 580 whined and yelped like caged lab animals awaiting dissection; but this part of Castro Valley Boulevard was big old frame houses that must have been here before World War II. Overlaid with hot-dog stands and drive-ins and laundromats and gas stations now, but with the old residential neighborhood still showing through like silver through the tarnish.

The rambling white house at 3877 had a lawn. It even had a garage instead of a carport. He walked across the grass just to feel it under his shoes; the back yard was full of roses. In the garage was an old Mercury whose license he didn't even bother to jot down.

He had stopped to eat, bringing twilight close enough

for lights to burn in the front room. The door was finally opened by a woman with iron-gray hair, of about the same vintage as the house. "Sorry I took so long; I was on the phone."

"I wonder if I might speak with Charles, ma'am."

"Chuck? My goodness, he hasn't lived here for—oh, seven, eight months anyway." She was vaguely horse-faced, with glasses, and surprisingly vigorous physical movements—which probably explained (and were explained by) that yardful of fantastic roses.

"Do you know where I might get in touch with him?"

"My goodness, no, I don't." She emphasized *don't;* it was a Midwest trick of speech, Illinois, Iowa, somewhere like that.

"I understood this was his mother's house."

"It was. She was my sister, you see, and . . ."

Which made her Mrs. Western. In the original investigation she had been contacted in Sacramento, where she had lived in a tract house. Once started, Harriet Western was a talker.

". . . still in escrow, but Marian *did* leave the house to Chuck, and in February he asked if I wanted to live in it. Just gave me the keys. Too many associations for him, he said. I moved in last month. He and his mother were *awfully* close, time he lived a life of his own. Over forty years old, big, fine-looking man—always was. Marian just *couldn't* let go . . ."

Big, fine-looking man. Big enough to bounce a blackjack off Bart's skull? Big enough, fine enough, to carry a 158-pound limp body into a basement garage, stuff it into a Jaguar, slide it over behind the wheel when the time came?

"When you say big, Mrs. Western . . ."

"Heavens, six feet tall, two hundred ten pounds now that he's lost all that weight. Was two hundred forty. And he lifts those barbell things around—he's strong as an ox. I remember . . ."

Better and better, Griffin looked. She hadn't seen him since the first week in February when he'd given her the keys, knew nothing of California Street in Concord.

Because of that Concord lead, Ballard had gone the seven miles east to the 680 Interstate interchange instead of doubling back through Oakland. Now he was zipping north through the valley in light traffic. Very good indeed, Griffin looked. Especially after Ballard had asked Harriet Western about the cash he'd understood her sister had left to Griffin.

"Cash? Cash money?" She'd given a hearty full-throated laugh. "She had this house free and clear, and that was *all*. Chuck's father was killed in a car accident in 1954, didn't leave her a dime of insurance. Chuck was the one giving *her* cash, not the other way around . . ."

Yeah, and Ballard had a pretty good idea where the cash had been coming from, too; at least during the past few years. Have to call JRS tomorrow, find out if an audit had been talked of *before* Griffin had taken off. He might have known his peculations had become gross enough so they would be caught when someone else went through the books, even if none of the partners realized it.

Charles M. Griffin, age forty-one, white, single, a middle-aged swinger driving the middle-aged swinger's car, the Thunderbird. And thief? And would-be murderer? And where, oh, where, are you, Chuckie-baby?

Meanwhile, Ballard, cool goddamn private eye, got lost.

Made it all the way up through Danville and Alamo and Walnut Creek (just beds of light laid down beside the raised 680 freeway) and then *stayed* on 680 when he should have veered right on California 242 just north of Pleasant Hill. He took the Concord Avenue off-ramp— the right street off the wrong freeway—and couldn't find California Street. Dammit, where the little residential grid was supposed to be laid down, there wasn't anything at all. Darkness. And beyond, where Concord was supposed to be, was a huge blare of lights that turned out to be an auto dealership with forty acres of used cars for sale. Then he ran out of gas, had to walk half a mile.

Shit, if he'd re-upped when his two years in the army were finished, he'd have been a sergeant by now. If he hadn't got his ass shot off in the meantime.

It was 9:07 P.M. when he turned off Concord Avenue into the old by-passed residential area on two-block California Street. He missed 1830 on the first drive-through, finally found it to be a low ranch-style plaster affair with a red asphalt shingle roof. The old-fashioned picket fence was almost bursting with roses even prettier than those in Castro Valley.

No garage; a dusty blue Bonneville with a white hardtop was parked in the weedy yard next to a tall elm. A rope hung from a convenient limb, knotted near the end so kids could use it to swing on. Cars were whipping by down on Concord Avenue in an angry blare of horns and headlights. Almost dark, but he could still see the outlines, beyond the old live oaks and the new multi-plexes, of the round-topped treeless California hills. The houses would climb them soon, too.

As he started through the weeds toward the front door, the lights went out. He paused. A woman came out, slamming the screen door behind her. She jumped and gasped when she saw him motionless in the yard.

"Jesus, you scared me, man!"

"I'm sorry. I'm trying to get hold of Griff, I thought you—"

"Griff?" The dying evening light showed her to be a big, buxom, dark-haired girl in her twenties. She wore skintight slacks over generous thighs; enough nipple poked against her red-and-white-striped T-shirt to show she wore no bra. Buxom was hardly the word. "Who the hell are you?"

"Ballard. You wouldn't know me, I'm from the city. Griff—"

"Get to hell out of my way," she said abruptly. She started to push past him. "I'm late for work."

Ballard put out a detaining hand. "I'm not on the make. I—"

"Keep your paws off me!"

A clawed hand came up at his eyes. Ballard caught her wrist, turned his body sideways in case she tried to knee him, but as soon as she pulled her wrist loose she went right on talking as if there had been no interruption.

"I'm sick of that bastard's rotten friends sucking around! This is *my* place now, get it? Next time I'll slap you with so much fuzz you'll be wearing stripes before you need a change of socks, believe me. They're my friends in this town."

Ballard seemed destined to never finish a sentence. "I'm not a *friend* of Griffin's, I'm a private—"

"*Buck* private, I suppose. Last one Griff brought around was so kinky he wanted me to sit on the edge of the bed so . . . oh, never mind!"

Ballard stared after her in the near-darkness, then burst out laughing. What else could he do? But he had learned something: the bounteously endowed girl apparently had moved in when Griffin had moved out. Or before. So the house was a rental, and rental properties meant landladies. Somewhere close by, perhaps? Like next door?

Next door it was, a well-kept house that looked pale green in the evening light, with a wood-shingle roof and attractive brown trim. A newly polished Galaxie-500 was parked in front under an evergreen. The woman who identified herself as the owner of 1830 wore gray slacks and a thin white blouse over a mannish frame that went with her sixtyish age. Heavy-rimmed glasses made her eyes owlish. Her name was Emily Tregum.

"Griffin? *Him?* He left in February, good riddance, six weeks after that car smash he had on Christmas Eve—"

"With the T-Bird?"

"That's right. They towed it away, should of kept it; but here a month later he had it back, all fixed up." She nodded her head in tart satisfaction. "Ask me, he's in jail—I know that's where he *should* be. Left owing over two hundred dollars in rent, besides selling all of my furniture from that house. Put an ad right in the newspaper."

"Do you know anyone who can put me in touch with him?"

She pursed meager lips, shook a finger at him in an oddly inappropriate gesture. "*Someone* bonded him over that auto wreck, then he jumped six hundred dollars' bail." She stopped, then added, "You look like a clean-cut young man, I'll tell you this. Cheri, the girl who rents from me now, used to know him."

"I, ah, just missed Cheri."

"Well, she works right down the street. On Concord Avenue." She leaned closer and lowered her voice. "In the topless place."

Ballard thanked her and turned to leave, then remembered another question. "Has anyone else been around asking about Griffin lately?"

"No," she said positively. " 'Less you count the Nigra man was around on, let's see, Tuesday it was. Told him just what I told you, 'cept about Cheri and all . . .'"

So Bart had been here. More to point to Griffin as the one. He said, "Why didn't you tell him about Cheri, ma'am?"

"Well, I *told* you. He was *colored*. He knew Cheri lives over there alone, he'd be after her, quick as scat. *They* can't help it, of course, but . . . well, he was eyeing *me* before I shut the door . . ."

The topless place was on the corner of Concord and Bonifacio, just being redone, so the outside walls were black tarpaper with chicken wire over them, waiting for the plasterers. The abbreviated gravel parking area held twelve autos, foreign and small and sporty except for one bright iridescent blue Continental, a peacock in a chicken coop.

Above the door in fancy neon script was Dukum Inn, with a sign under it, TOPLESS, in big red painted letters, with NOW underneath that in smaller black letters.

Ballard went through the heavy door, leathered and brass-studded on the inside. It was jammed. A lot of couples and even more single men, young, the sort that wear their hair too long and comb it incessantly by the back-bar mirror. In back, where in less frenetic times a shuffleboard would have been, was a stage. On it was a four-man combo, and gyrating wildly in front of them, wearing nothing but brief panties and flying sweat, was Cheri, the girl from 1830. Her bared breasts lived up to their promise under the striped T-shirt.

"What'll it be, sir?"

"Just a beer." Ballard didn't take his eyes from the girl and her heavy jouncing bust. No wonder she was so defensive; in a place like this, a lot of hands would have been reaching for that candy.

"Same price as whiskey, y'know," warned the bartender absently, staring beyond him at Cheri with complacent lust.

"That's okay, I'm driving. Ah . . . how many girls do you have?"

"Just the two. Her an' Cleo. Ain't she somethin'? Cheri Tart."

Ballard opened his mouth, realized it was open, and shut it again. Cheri Tart. How would he cover that in his report? Topless, dying in the city, seemed very big—in several ways—in Concord.

"Griff been around lately?" he asked, very casually.

"Chuck Griffin?" He shook his head slowly, side-to-side, his eyes moving in their sockets so they stayed fixed on the stage. "Not for three, four months, anyway."

"Hell! I've been at sea since the first of the year, just got in. Owe him some money and . . . Hey!" He let a light dawn in his eye. "Wasn't he going out with one of these girls here or something? Sure! *That* girl. Cheri." He picked up his glass and beer, turned toward a table a foursome was just vacating. "Tell her I'm here with Griff's twenty bucks. She'll recognize me."

Ten minutes later she threaded her way directly to his table, wearing her slacks and T-shirt, barefoot and sullen-faced, slapping away eager hands. Behind her the combo was belting out, of all things, a bad rendition of the old Johnny Cash "Ring of Fire." She pulled out the chair across from Ballard and flopped in it with a huge sigh.

"What the hell, it's a living," he told her discontented face. He laid a twenty on the table.

She laughed suddenly, then tapped the bill with a long red fingernail. In a moment of intense sexual fantasy, Ballard's imagination felt the fingernail running languidly down his bare spine.

"This doesn't buy you anything," she said.

"What I said at the house was the truth, Cheri. I'm not on the make. I'm just trying to get in touch with Griffin."

"A sweet guy," she said unexpectedly. Her eyes were very clear under their tremendous overlay of mascara. "On the sauce too heavy, but a sweet guy. Gentle. And square, y'know? A real thing about his mother. Sometimes I think he dug me because I've got these big titties." She put a hand under one of them and flopped it once, casually, as if it were a cow's udder. "Like, the big mother image or something, y'know?"

"What was all this about kinky—"

"That was the other guy. Griff, he was strictly missionary-style." She held her joined hands out, palms together as if in prayer but with the hands horizontal, not vertical, with the left on the bottom. She began rocking the right by raising the heel while the fingertips remained pressed to those of the left. It was almost shockingly graphic. "Like that, y'know? Always. Me Tarzan, you Jane." Her eyes got a faraway look. "But a sweet guy."

The combo paused after scattered clapping. Then a rebel yell went up as Cleo appeared.

"If he was so sweet, what happened?"

"He just took off." She snapped her fingers. "Like that. We had a big fight over this other guy—"

"The kinky one?"

"That's him." She suddenly shuddered. "Tall, good-looking guy. Griff brought him in to see me dance. February eighth it was, I remember it 'cause it was one month to the day after I moved in with Griff. Anyway, we all got loaded between gigs. At one o'clock the three of us went back up to the house and Griff went out for a bottle. This clown dragged me right into the bedroom like he owned me, y'know?" Her eyes were indignant. "Tore the pantyhose right off me, four-ninety-eight a pair, and you know what he wanted? To look up me. Honest. With a flashlight."

Ballard had trouble keeping his face straight. "You let him?"

"No. I kicked him—where it hurts, even if you're barefooted. Then I ran out. I slept over to my girl friend's where I roomed before I went in with Griff. He came over the next morning, Griff, and I really lit into him. This guy came on so *strong,* I thought he *had* to have been told I was an easy lay or something, y'know? Real kinky guy. Griff felt terrible about it, he had no idea. Said he was gonna do something about it . . ."

Ballard nodded. "So when I showed up tonight—"

"Yeah. I thought, just like the other one." She put out her hand impulsively. "I'm not that bitchy usually, honest."

"What I don't understand, if Griff was such a nice guy, why he just took off like that."

"Yeah, how do you like that?" Cheri asked broodily, eyes dark with remembered injustice. "The next day, after we fought and made up so I thought everything was fine, he goes off to work and just keeps going. Walks out without a word. And then the next week guys start coming in, hauling out the furniture right from under me! Honest. Said they'd bought it from Griff, left checks made out to him. Finally, like three weeks or a month later —maybe early March or something—here comes this phone call from him."

"Phone call?" asked Ballard almost sharply.

"From a bar somewhere," she nodded. "He's about half shit-face, y'know? The music so loud I can hardly hear him. Says he's sorry it didn't work out, would I, like, mail these checks for the furniture to him. I was pretty sore at the time, y'know, but I got something else going for myself now. Might even marry him, big deal."

Ballard rubbed his jaw, hard. He said cautiously, "Ah . . . you wouldn't remember that address you mailed the checks to, would you?"

"No. But I got it up to the house. I'll run up and get it for you on my next break."

The address was 1545 Midfield Road. In San Jose. Ballard felt it was worth his twenty bucks.

Twelve

It wasn't. It was a tract house and it was empty. Empty, by the look of it, for quite a while. The streetlight behind Ballard showed bare living-room walls and floors; the cheap ornamental mailbox on the porch was empty. Garage locked but empty. So much for 1545 Midfield Road in San Jose. Twenty DKA bucks down the tubes (if Kearny would even honor the payment), a forty-mile drive from Concord for nothing, another sixty to get back to San Francisco.

And when he got there, he still had to positively eliminate Hemovich—which wouldn't get him any closer to Charles M. Griffin.

Before leaving, Ballard wrote down the numbers of the houses on either side and of the three across the street. This would give the skip-tracers something to work with. He took the new inner route, Interstate 280, a great beautiful stretch of freeway which ran up the spine of the peninsula behind the bedroom communities cupped between the coast and the Bay. It was an almost exhilarating drive; the highway was starkly deserted, he fled north with the radio blaring and the window wide to let stinging fresh air slap at his tired face. Despite an unfinished stretch near the Crystal Spring Reservoir, he took the Alemany off-ramp near the Farmer's Market at 1:10 A.M.

Twenty-five hours left to Kearny's deadline, and not a damned thing proved. Lots of eliminating, but no proof *of* anything.

As he had hoped, the Roadrunner was parked in the

driveway on Nevada Street, its nose against the gimmicked garage door. He parked around the corner at the bottom of the hill, on Crescent, and walked up. Usually, once he had gotten into it, he would have rolled the car downhill and out of sight of the house before starting it. But this time he doggedly ran the Chrysler pop keys on it right there. The third one he worked in the lock with delicate fingers did it. The radio screamed hard rock until he found the right button to punch it silent; the overhead light wouldn't go off even when he shut the door.

Ballard revved the engine, turned to look over his shoulder as he backed it out. And looked right into the face of a red-headed woman outside the door. He was so startled he killed it. She tapped with a knuckle, mouthed the word "Please" through the glass. He rolled down the window, recklessly—a field agent named Warner once had caught a three-pound can of coffee right in the face that way.

"I just want to get our possessions out of it," she said. She had very pale skin and a narrow, small-featured face that looked much younger than her age. Despite the hour, she was fully made-up.

"Be my guest."

She delved in the glove box, pulled papers from above the visor. "Lying about who you were on the phone," she said disdainfully. She was dressed in a rather faded quilted robe and fuzzy red slippers, a get-up far from sexy. People.

"It worked," said Ballard. He added, almost casually, "I have to know where you and lover-boy were on Tuesday night, too."

"You've got a lot of nerve!" she blazed. "If you think—"

"Me or the police. Take your pick."

"We haven't done . . ." She paused, shivered, said, "What time Tuesday night?" She eased in on the seat beside him, face almost haggard, as if impelled by her own obscure feelings of guilt.

"You tell me."

"We were having a row with my mother and brother up

in San Rafael until after midnight. I know it was one-thirty when we got back here."

Say, 12:30 leaving San Rafael. If that checked out, they were clear. And having talked to Virginia Pressler, he couldn't see her as helping anyone attempt murder.

"Who won the fight?"

"Oh God, it was terrible! They just don't understand. Mom—" She stopped abruptly, a surprised look on her face.

Ballard reached over, took the keys to the Roadrunner from her unresisting fingers. The fingers were icy cold. He said, "Leave him. Go back to your old man."

"How dare you! I ought to . . ." Her face contorted suddenly; she started crying, turned to Ballard and jammed her head, hard, against his chest like a little girl. "Oh God," she sobbed into his shirt collar, "what am I going to do?"

"Keep him away from your old man for openers," said Ballard literally. "He's got a loaded shotgun and he's just waiting."

"Oh God!" she said again. She got out, stood there in a listening attitude, as if hoping for some revelation that would magically unsnarl the tangle of her life.

Ballard had no revelations; all he could offer was a monosyllable. "Luck," he said; and meant it.

When he parked the Ford and turned off the ignition, silence trilled in his ears like phone wires strung across empty winter fields. After 3:00 A.M. He stayed slumped behind the wheel for a full minute, literally too tired to move. Finally he groaned, got out, locked the car. The ocean-laden air swirled early-summer fog around him, haloing the streetlights. The 800 block of Lincoln Way was deserted. Across the street a hedge hid the wide darkness of Golden Gate Park.

Turning from the car, he lost his balance like a drunk, had to steady himself with a hand on the fender. Shot. Utterly shot. And on his desk, when he had brought in the Roadrunner, had been a note he was to be in at eight o'clock to knock heads with Kearny on the investigation to date.

Right now, twenty-three hours left. For him; perhaps for Bart. Jesus. He crossed the sidewalk to the old narrow pink house; he had the downstairs front, two rooms with a phonied-up cubicle of a kitchen and a bathroom and shower down the hall which he shared with the Japanese couple in the rear.

As he started up the front steps, a car door slammed and rapid female steps clipped the sidewalk behind him. He turned, hollow-eyed. "Corinne! What . . ." Then her presence shocked him wide awake. He caught her by the arms. "Bart! What? Is Bart? Is—"

"Get your hands off me, white boy!" she blazed. He stepped back in confusion. Her full dark lips curled in a smile that was nearly a sneer. She was wearing a fawn-colored coat that buttoned up high under the chin in a complicated strap-and-brass-button arrangement. "What would you say if I told you he was gone?"

"Is . . ." The fear crowded his heart like an embolism. "Is . . ."

"No. If layin' there like a lump of gray shit is all right, he's still all right." Her lips curled again; her accent was blatantly Negro, something that, like Bart, she could assume at will. "Had you worried there for a minnit, white boy?"

Ballard sat down abruptly on the cold steps, like a gunnysack full of seed tipping over. He shook his head. "For Christ sake, Corinne," he protested weakly. Then he added, "Did you have to wait long? I—"

"Don't matter 'bout black girl waitin', black girl wait all afternoon, all night at the hospital. Waitin' for the white mutha to show."

He didn't blame her for being sore, but he was so god-*damn* tired. And tomorrow he had to keep pushing, had to *really* push tomorrow. He blew out a long breath. "Okay, kid. I'm sorry. I was over in the East Bay, I got tied up." Adrenalin stirred at the thought. "I know which one did it."

"What you care *who* dunnit, white boy? What you care—"

"That's stopped being cute, Corinne."

"Ain't meant to be cute, white boy." Her voice was still tight and hard, her smile a rictus beneath glittering eyes. "You oughta see yo'se'f in a mirror sometime. *Biiig* man. *Tough* man. Hard an' ruthless an' no time for nothin' but mountie-gets-his-man jive . . ."

He stood up to take her wrists, to shake her gently like a child. "Corinne! Stop it!"

"Okay," she said soberly, in her normal voice. "All through."

A single burst of traffic went by, released by a green light at Ninth Avenue.

"You've *got* to get some rest, Corinne, you're on the ragged edge."

She peered up at him, nodding dutifully, then suddenly leaned closer. Her eyes sharpened. "And *you* have to keep working," she crooned softly. She was staring at him by the dim vestibule light. "You're a detective, have to detect, no time to come to the hospital, that's only logical. Got to get the one did it to Bart . . ." She raised her eyes to his face; the eyes were enormous and tired and defeated, but her voice was mockingly black in dialect. "Wanna take me inside fo' a trick, white man? Want some nigger meat? My stud liable to die, gotta get me some—"

"Corinne!"

Her voice was soft and deadly. "You should've wiped off the lipstick—honky!"

She swung a fisted hand with all her strength; he rolled with it, so it caught the side of his neck instead of his face. His shoe slipped on the mist-slicked stair tread, he went down on his side, saving himself from a fall down the steps only by skinning a palm against the bricks flanking the entryway.

"Corinne!" he cried.

But she was already across the sidewalk, into the old black Triumph, jabbing the starter as he came off the steps. The little car shot away from the curb in a shriek of tires, was a third of a block away before the lights went on. He ran a few paces toward his own car, stopped.

That goddamn Virginia Pressler and her goddamn lipstick. Corinne had thought he'd been shacked up instead of working. Fiercely, intensely loyal to her man. And now, between her and Ballard, the whole stupid silly racial thing, like something the cat had thrown up on the rug. If he followed her, got it all explained, no sleep at all tonight. No sleep, when tomorrow he had to dig as he'd never dug before, had to dig out a dead skip who'd gone underground, had eluded DKA for three months already.

Cursing bitterly, Ballard went inside and went to bed.

Thirteen

It was 9:37 A.M. Fridays were always busy, with the banks open until six o'clock, and all the paper work to clear up before the weekend. Too damned much paper work, most of it waste motion just to satisfy the state. Yesterday, two hours arguing premiums with the insurance company. Last evening, another hour spent looking over that property on Eleventh Street yet again. Too crowded here at Golden Gate, that was the truth.

Dan Kearny took an impatient turn around the cubicle, ran a hand through his graying hair, stared with distaste at the mountains of files on the desk.

Gray hair. And billing. Hell, he ought to be glad that he had the business to bill.

His pleasantly tough, slightly battered face, with the nose just a bit awry from a fist or a bottle or a steering wheel—depending on which story he was telling that week—suddenly brightened. Come in tomorrow, the office was quiet on Saturdays, get the work out. Which would mean that today . . .

He bent over the desk, lit a cigarette as he buzzed Giselle on the intercom. "Let's take a ride," he said when she answered.

Outside, he stood on the sidewalk with his arms folded, his cigarette drifting smoke up into the morning overcast which would lift by noon.

Right here, Wednesday morning, Heslip had gotten it. No doubt about that; and after the carefully detailed hour with Ballard this morning, not a hell of a lot of doubt about who had done it. Griffin. Looked tired as hell, Ballard, carrying his head as if he had a stiff neck from the clout Corinne Jones apparently had given him. Well, being tired didn't hurt field agents. Kearny had never minded the all-night, round-the-clock, week-long sessions he'd put in himself in the thirty years since he'd started grabbing cars for old man Walters as a tough kid of fourteen.

Kearny grinned to himself at the memory, then thought: Where the hell *is* that girl? You spent half your life waiting for some woman or another. He threw away his butt and shook out another cigarette.

Wild and woolly days then, five bucks a repo, investigate on your own time. Weekends, fighting club stags until he'd enlisted at sixteen, lying about his age and getting away with it. Probably one of the reasons he'd always had such a soft spot for Bart Heslip.

Well, times had changed.

But the subjects hadn't. People still defrauded, defaulted, embezzled—money or goods or chattels. They cheated their employers or their wives, skipped out, dropped out of sight, just plain dropped out. Skid row or hippie commune, juice, pills, grass, acid, skin-popping or mainlining skag—the old-time cons had used a better name for the white stuff, shit.

It usually came down to money. Somebody wanted more than he had, or wanted what it could buy. Somebody else would spend some to get back his chattels, or his missing daughter, or the embezzler who had nickle-and-dimed the books (Griffin, at least, thought big).

And you went after them—for money. You found them, most of them. Damned tough to stay out of the way of an agency like DKA if it really wanted you. You had to change your name, dye your hair, keep your kids out of school, quit your union or your profession, tear up your credit cards, abandon your wife, not show up at your mother's funeral, run your car into a deep river, quit paying taxes, get off welfare.

Because every habit pattern was a doorway into your life, a doorway that the skip-tracers and field agents with the right key could open. The right clue, he supposed, in the detective-story sense.

A few made it, of course, the dead skips who became invisible men. Charles M. Griffin had done it so far, might have done it indefinitely if he hadn't ventured out to clip Bart Heslip over the head.

Now they had him outside the burrow, were running him hard.

Giselle came down the stairs, long lovely legs flashing under the hem of her fashionably short skirt.

"I'm sorry, Dan. Todd from the bank was on the phone."

"Problems?"

They began walking down Franklin toward Kearny's parked Galaxy wagon with the long whippet aerial. Giselle shook her head, made a face that emphasized little smile lines at the corners of her mouth which would have been dimples in a fleshier face.

"No problems. Todd didn't get his promotion to V-P, and was looking for someone to hold his hand."

Kearny opened the rider's door for her; the tall blonde slid in past him in another flash of wickedly long shapely legs. Kearny was aware of her as a woman, but only as it related to her ability to do her job. She'd started out typing skip-letters while she was still in high school, now had her own license and wasn't far behind Kearny himself in understanding what the detective business was all about.

As for making a pass at her, he'd as soon have made one at his own five-year-old daughter. Sex was for home, and maybe sometimes for a convention where the booze snuck up on you and knocked your judgment awry.

"Where are we going, Dan'l?" Her eyes sparkled; getting out of the office was rare enough to be a treat.

"First to the hospital, to see Bart."

She instantly sobered. "Will he make it?"

"He'll make it." His voice carried utter conviction; no way to tell whether it was mere ritual or was really believed.

Kearny went up Franklin, eyes busy on license plates.

He had a phenomenal memory for plate numbers, probably spotted more cars off the skip-list than all the field men put together.

"How was your session with Larry this morning?"

"You've been reading his reports?" When she nodded, he went on, "He knocked them off one by one, a beautiful job."

"All except friend Griffin." Unconsciously, she repeated his own thought of a few minutes before. "The invisible man. Think Larry'll connect before your deadline?"

"He's busting his back trying."

He parked on Bush just off Divisadero; they got on the big, slow, lumbering elevator inside the hospital's rear ambulance entrance.

"This is the first time you've been here, isn't it, Dan?"

He nodded. "No sense in sitting around staring at a man in coma."

"Corinne Jones wouldn't agree."

"Corinne Jones wouldn't agree if I said black was beautiful."

In the room they found the same scene Ballard had, except that the drapes were pulled back to let in some light. Bart's eyes were closed, but Kearny noted the tracheal tube was gone from the windpipe. Glucose dripped from an upside-down bottle suspended above the bed.

"Has there been any change at all?" asked Giselle.

But Corinne Jones, rising from her chair beside the bed, seemed to see only Kearny. Her face quirked in a sneer Ballard would have recognized from the night before. "Well, well, well! Sherlock Holmes! The great man himself!"

Kearny looked at her for a moment. He rubbed the side of his nose. He turned to Giselle and said, "Why don't you go see if you can find Dr. Whitaker."

"Oh, you're so smooth!" exclaimed Corinne. "So bland! You pay for a private room, you think that absolves you of—"

"He should be somewhere around the hospital this time of day," said Kearny inexorably, his heavy voice overriding Corinne's. He'd never learned how to back off from anything, including upset women.

When Giselle hesitated, stiff-faced, Corinne said in her tight furious voice, "He's gonna whup the nigger, don't you see? He don't want any witnesses."

Giselle went, fast enough so it was just short of fleeing. Her face was white. She'd never been able to handle personal emotions stripped of their insulation.

Kearny looked blandly at the black girl, his hard square face completely without expression, his gray eyes opaque as a snake's. "Now, what seems to be troubling you, Miss Jones?"

She told him, at length. Some of it was four-letter, some of it inchoate, some of it obscene, some brilliant, some silly. All of it was cathartic. She paused for breath, her eyes flashing and her fine full bosom heaving beneath the fuzzy beige sweater she wore.

"Have a cigarette," suggested Kearny.

She burst out crying.

He lit up, went to the head of the bed to stare down at Heslip. When she began working on her eyes with her handkerchief, he said, as if he could see her with his back turned, "What it boils down to is that I'm a son of a bitch for giving Bart a job."

"That isn't a job, it's a disease! All of you—scavengers! Picking on the poor and the out-of-luck and the defenseless—"

Kearny turned to look at her. "Bullshit," he said pleasantly.

"You wouldn't say that to me if I was a white woman!" she cried.

Kearny leaned across the bed, talking in a sudden harsh tight voice that drove her back by its very intensity. "Did you ever stop to think just how goddamn sick guys like me get of that black beauty, black power, downtrodden blacks crap? My people didn't keep slaves, lady. They came over here in a cattle boat back around the turn of the century. I don't hire people because of their color. Bart works for me because he's damn good at what he does. Period."

"What he does is brutalizing."

"What about keeping what you don't pay for? Stealing credit cards? Ripping off companies that sell things people need? Embezzling? Pilfering cargoes you're hired to unload? Cheating on welfare? These are uplifting? The rotten bastard who did this—he's a poor misunderstood little feller who had to hit Bart because he used to piss the bed at night? Grow up."

Corinne said, in an almost normal voice, "Then you *do* believe that it wasn't just an accident!"

"I . . ." It stopped him dead for a moment. Women, there was just *no* way to ever tell what they were going to come up with. He fought back a grin. He said, "I believe it. And I'm going to get the son of a bitch who did it."

"Larry's going to get him, not you! You can't even give him another man to help him work those cases."

After clouting Ballard alongside the head a few hours before. He smiled bleakly. "Speaking of Ballard, keep your hands off him. He's walking around with his head on one side like he's just gone a fast ten with Clay." He made an abrupt elaborate bow. "Pardon me. Ali."

"Go to hell," she said. But the corners of her mouth were trying to quirk. Good stuff in her; she just had too short a fuse.

The door opened and Giselle came in, followed by mod little Whitaker. He came only about breast-high on the tall blonde, but seemed to be enjoying the view at that level. Today he was a symphony of red, green, and pale blue, which made him look remarkably like a Fillmore Street pimp. All he needed was Tiger's razor, Kearny thought.

"Sounded like a lively discussion in here," he beamed.

"Looks like another nice day, Doc," said Kearny in his crushingly bland voice.

At the JRS Garage, Giselle stayed in the car while Kearny went in. Leo Busilloni was there, much as Ballard had described him, along with Danny Walker, the senior of the three partners. Like Leo, he wore white coveralls;

it was not a company where the executives sat around handling correspondence.

"What I don't understand is why he moved to San Jose," said Leo. He said it as if Kearny had just made an indecent suggestion to him.

"I doubt if he ever did."

"I don't follow that." Danny had a broken-grating whiskey voice and was smoking a vile stogie that looked like a sawed-off shotgun. "Your man was *at* the house last night, you say . . ."

"Misdirection, I think," said Kearny. "There was no reason for him to call up the topless dancer and give her the address if all he wanted to say was that he wouldn't be seeing her again."

"He wanted the cash from selling the landlady's furniture," said Leo promptly.

Kearny shook his head. "I guess, but it sounds almost like he was doing it for spite. It sure as hell makes no sense in relation to an embezzlement—but *without* an embezzlement, and a damned big one, nothing *else* he's done since February makes sense . . ."

Which should have been that. He had passed on the information about the will not being out of probate, as Ballard had asked, had also learned that no audit had been planned previous to Griffin's disappearance. They wouldn't even be planning one now if Elkin hadn't insisted after getting stuck with Griffin's job and seeing how screwed up the records seemed.

Back at the office, he sat down to the billing while Giselle went back upstairs. Five minutes later he was on his feet again, pacing. Corinne Jones had been right, he *hadn't* given Ballard much help in finding Griffin. If there were *two* men in the field, working different addresses simultaneously, DKA could pick that bastard's nose for him a lot sooner. Maybe even within Kearny's phony deadline. Yes, two good field men . . .

It never occurred to Kearny that DKA might *not* turn Griffin. Hell, he'd been in town Wednesday morning, hadn't he? Which meant that he had left tracks, somewhere in the Bay Area.

Kearny called Giselle on the intercom. "Type me up an assignment sheet on Griffin. I'll contact Larry direct once I'm on the other side of the Oakland hills where he can pick me up. Don't alert Oakland Control that I'll be in their area; I'm available only for the Griffin case today."

Giselle quickly typed up a duplicate case assignment on Charles M. Griffin; she realized she was humming while she did it. *Now* Larry Ballard was going to find out what work was. And digging. And hanging in there until a case broke. Kearny was moving in. Which meant it was going to be a long hard day today, a long hard night tonight—and little Giselle was going to be sitting right here on the squawk box taking the whole thing in.

Because these were the hours she lived for: when the jaws began to close.

Fourteen

When Ballard had hit the East Bay that morning, he hadn't known that Kearny would be in the field before noon. He didn't know anything about closing jaws, or care. He'd spent the drive over picking at the deadline, only fifteen hours away, and at the fact that he was no closer to Griffin than he had ever been. Another thing that niggled: he had forgotten to mention either to Kearny or in his report that the T-Bird had been in a wreck in December. Not that it made much difference; the car had been on the street since then.

Was Kearny going to take him off the case tonight after the deadline passed, if he hadn't turned Griffin by that time? Then Ballard would have to quit DKA and go on his own. Especially after last night with Corinne. The only way he'd ever square things with her was to have the son of a bitch standing beside the bed in handcuffs when Bart woke up. *If* Bart woke up. Dammit, Bart *had* to wake up.

And meanwhile, he still had today. Had to think the way Kearny would think, work the leads the way Kearny would work them. He still remembered Kearny on the Mayfield case, when Ballard had been with DKA for only a month, taking apart a welfare worker named Vikki Goodrich to get an address. And later, after Jocelyn Mayfield had killed herself and Ballard had wanted to quit the detective business, going after Ballard the same way.

*What will you do now, Ballard—go home and cry into
your pillow? She's going to be dead for a long, long time.*

What would he do if *Bart* died? Or ended up with a
fifty-card deck?

He was doing it. Running down the bastard responsible.

The Concord police department and municipal court
shared quarters at Willow Pass Road and Parkside Avenue. Ballard passed the Dukum Inn en route. In daylight
it looked old and shrunken and dispirited, like an aging
swinger getting up in the morning with his teeth still in
the water glass. In front of the white-plaster court building
were spaces reserved for police and sheriff's deputies, and
a few green fifteen-minute meters for people paying parking fines. Ballard U-turned to a one-hour meter across the
street. Since Emily Tregum had suggested Griffin might be
in jail, he had to check.

The desk sergeant was red-headed and Ballard's age,
with freckles on his nose and the backs of his hands; he
should have used Scope that morrning.

"I'm sorry, sir, we can't give out arrest records here. I
would suggest you try at the Contra Costa county jail
over in Martinez. If this Griffin is in jail there now, they'll
tell you."

"Do you have any records of an auto accident that
involved Griffin last Christmas Eve?"

A girl wearing hair curlers and very hot hotpants came
in to lean on the counter next to Ballard, unabashedly
listening to them. She was twenty pounds overweight for
even lukewarm hotpants.

"This was in Concord?" asked the cop.

"I think so."

Coming back with a folder a few minutes later, the
desk sergeant veered over to the far end of the counter
from the overweight girl.

"Nosy little drip," he said in a cheerfully quiet voice
when Ballard joined him. "December twenty-fourth, a
two-car accident with a vehicle driven by a Miss Wanda
Moher."

"You have an address on her?"

"Let's see, a . . . 3-6-8-1 Willow Pass Road, Concord."

"Thanks a lot, Officer." Ballard started to turn away, then remembered to ask, "Was anyone cited in that?"

"Your friend Griffin. Drunk driving, violation-of-right-of-way. His trial was scheduled for last February eleventh; what the outcome was I don't know."

As Ballard went out the door, the cop already was turning to the overweight, underdressed girl, automatically reaching under the counter for a complaint form. In one of the reserved-for-police spaces was a maroon and white Mustang with the driver's window open and the key in the ignition. Ballard repressed a shudder. She was going to make someone a dreadful wife one of these days.

The Hacienda Apartments were double-tiered around an open inner court, like a motel, California ersatz and instant stylish, individualized as canned martinis. Across Willow Pass Road, towering far beyond the intersecting patterns of TV aerials and high power lines, were the serrated smog-dimmed outlines of Mount Diablo. Ballard wondered what it had been like here when it was only rolling empty golden hills.

The mailboxes were set against the oh-so-rustic redwood slat fence which shielded the fishbowl-sized swimming pool. Wanda Moher was not listed. He found a door in the fence under a sign reading *Manager,* went through. *Manager* seemed at first to be a trio of yapping miniature poodles; then a birdlike woman in shorts with desperately skinny yet flaccid legs appeared behind them in the screened doorway. She chirped at them, cawed at Ballard.

"Wanda Moher moved out three days ago." She craned over his head at the second tier of apartments across the court. "Eighteen-C, two over from the head of the stairs. She came in half an hour ago to get the rest of her stuff, she might still be there."

Exteriors were pale-pink stucco with red-tiled roofs; interiors were bland as oatmeal, computer-designed so everything was built in except the tenants. Wanda was a very short, quite pretty girl who could not have weighed over ninety pounds, standing in the middle of the littered room with the dazed look of a homeowner after the fire engines have departed. Her straight nose and long straight upper lip gave her a surprisingly rabbitlike face.

"I've never met a real detective before," she said, "but I *love* Agatha Christie . . ."

Ballard, who only read Richard Stark, said he was looking for a Mr. Charles M. Griffin. The transformation in Wanda Moher was startling. Her eyes flashed as much as a rabbit's eyes *can* flash.

"I hope he's in trouble good! Anything I can do to help you . . ."

"Start with the accident," he suggested.

It was only 11:30 in the morning, Christmas Eve morning to be exact, and she was driving down to Oakland for some last-minute shopping. Her mother . . . Anyway, here came Griffin, completely drunk, zooming out of this parking lot beside a *bar,* and . . .

"That would be the Dukum Inn?" Ballard asked, on a hunch.

"Gee, it's got a reputation with you fellows, huh?" Then her eyes got very big and she nodded wisely. "Of course! *Topless!*"

Her car had sustained over four hundred dollars' worth of damage—the subject's third such offense in less than four months. The police, she said, had told her they were determined to get him off the road this time.

"Did he lose his license at the February court date?"

"He never showed up. His lawyer got some sort of continuance for more time or something until next month. But the man who put up the money for his bond or whatever it was had to pay up. In cash."

"Do you know who that would be?" asked Ballard.

She shrugged, momentarily outlining small, very pointed breasts under her pale pastel blouse. "Maybe my insurance agent would know. His name is Harvey E. Wyman and he's right here in Concord."

At 1820 Mount Diablo Boulevard, as a matter of fact. She knew because it was right next door to Moneyfast Finance, where her mother had a loan. She could be reached in future at her mother's house at 1799 LaCalle Street, in that subdivision out beyond . . .

One-fifteen. And breakfast had been a cup of the DKA office coffee, which always tasted as if someone had brewed a dead rat in it. And of course they'd been out of Pream. They were always out of Pream. Somebody, probably Kearny, kept an empty jar there to fool you, but Ballard could never remember ever having found anything in it. Unless that was where they kept the rat between pots.

Since 1820 Mount Diablo Boulevard was less than three miles from Miss Moher's non-stop mouth, he would check it before lunch. He doubted if the insurance agent would know very much—his name, maybe, if he was having a good day—but it was worth a stop.

It was a very bright and sunny two-person office, decorated in primary colors. Wyman's empty desk was in the back by the wide picture window. At a much smaller desk in the center of the room a pleasant-faced middle-aged woman was talking on the phone. When she was finished, Ballard learned that Mr. Wyman was expected back within the hour. She would not feel right about going into Miss Moher's file without Mr. Wyman's knowledge and permission. He *did* understand?

Ballard understood. "I'll grab a sandwich and be back in—oh, thirty, forty minutes."

That would be fine. There was a coffee shop around the corner on Concord Boulevard. The cheeseburger and fries he had were so incredibly bad—even the pickle was soggy—that he was partially prepared for the coffee. But only partially. After tasting it, he really expected to find a tadpole in the bottom of his cup.

When he caught himself falling asleep over it, he went out to the car to bring in the Griffin file to review. A hole became immediately apparent. He'd forgotten to check at the Concord courthouse when he had been at the police department. He would go back there after he'd finished with Wyman, find out who the bail bondsman was who'd gotten burned, get the name of Griffin's lawyer.

After that, to Martinez to check the county jail. Drop in at the Dukum Inn to find out about the accident in December. Maybe get the name of the garage where the T-Bird had been towed; that really ought to be in the file even though it was meaningless information.

And after that . . .

Ballard shook his head. He was starting to feel a little panicky. About twelve hours left, he was really just making motions, spinning his wheels. He didn't have anywhere else to go.

But that did remind him to stop at his car and call KFS 499, Oakland Control, so they could call Giselle over in S.F. Yes, the San Jose field agent had been out to Midfield Road this morning. None of the neighbors had ever seen the subject around the address, but a T-Bird, red with a white hardtop, had been parked in the garage for several weeks in February and March. Nobody remembered the license, of course.

The tract home had been rented from the realty office by phone, paid for by a cashier's check depositing six months' rent in a lump sum. The transmitter of the check: Charles M. Griffin. The six months would be up on August 10, which meant it had been rented on February 10. A day before the court date he hadn't shown up for, according to Wanda Moher. San Jose had done a hell of a job on short notice. But what did it add up to? What was bugging him?

Ballard got out of the car, then paused. Car. That was it. Why had Griffin quit paying for the T-Bird? He'd had plenty of cash, siphoned from JRS Garage. Why rent a house in San Jose to store the T-Bird in the garage with money he could have put into the car payments?

Harvey E. Wyman was red-faced and jovial and midthirties, and should have taken up jogging the year before. He was also, unlike so many small insurance agents Ballard had met, very sharp. Very sharp indeed.

"Oh, I remember that Griffin accident, all right. Much better than I would like to. Three hundred bucks damage to his car, over four hundred to Wanda's . . ."

"Who was his insurance company?"

Wyman looked up from the Moher file the secretary had laid on his desk. "He was driving without any. Our people had to eat the loss on Wanda's car."

"They're suing, of course?"

"We've never been able to find him to serve him." He went back to the file. "Jumped bail in February, didn't show in municipal court . . ."

"What address did you show on him at that time?"

"Eighteen-hundred-something California Street, here in town. But I have a later one than that—"

"Midfield Road in San Jose? We have that. We—"

"No, this is here in Concord . . ." Ballard straightened up, his heart pumping. Wyman nodded. "Here it is. You see, I have my own repair work done at the same garage that fixed up the T-Bird after the December smash. They worked on it again last month . . ."

Ballard snapped, "He was sure it was the same car?"

"Oh, sure. He showed me the work order, same license number. The address was 1377 Mount Diablo Street . . ."

Ballard was halfway across the office, throwing a hurried "Thanks" over his shoulder, when Wyman called him back. "I rushed a process server out there, but hell, the people living there had never heard of Griffin."

"They could have been lying—"

Wyman shrugged. "I've used this guy for years, he's tough to lie to. It's a family: husband, wife, couple of kids. No connection with Griffin at all. I guess he just picked the address out of a phone book."

Hell, it *had* to have some meaning, Ballard thought. Mount Diablo Street, as opposed to Boulevard, was just a block away, 1377 just a few blocks west. It was a live one, he could *feel* it was a live one. He left rubber in front of Harvey E. Wyman's office.

Fifteen

At 1:45 P.M., just as Ballard sank a hesitant tooth into his soggy cheeseburger in Concord, Dan Kearny parked his station wagon on Main Street in Martinez. He still hadn't been able to raise Ballard on the radio. Field agents working addresses in a constricted area were in and out of their cars like yo-yos; eventually he would catch him. Meanwhile, he had a pretty good idea of what Ballard was doing.

Kearny's first stop on reaching the East Bay had been, like Ballard's, the Concord police department. The inelegant rear in the striped hotpants had long since wobbled out—to a ten-buck parking tag, a fact to warm Ballard's heart—but the freckled desk sergeant still was available. He repeated his information to Kearny, and added, on request, an excellent verbal of Ballard.

"You should have been a cop," Kearny dead-panned.

He went around the corner to the municipal court, which Ballard had missed. A short hall ended in wide double doors leading to the courtroom of the presiding judge. On one of them was a typed notice dated February 17, detailing acceptable dress for court appearances. Barefoot was not acceptable, nor were hotpants. Long hair and beards carried no interdictions short, it could be assumed, of nesting sparrows.

Kearny went back down the hall to a Dutch door with the top half open on a room containing four women and a great many file-jammed open-face cabinets. The ladies were huddled by the windows, gabbing.

"Where do I find out about docketings?" Kearny asked.

"Right here."

"Griffin, Charles M."

One of the women found the applicable clipboard and, with another, checked it. Both of them were placid as cattle, but Kearny evinced no impatience. He was in the field, working. You kept going, you kept digging, until you got there. It was as simple as that.

"No record here, sir."

"Has anyone else been around asking about Griffin within the last three hours?"

She immediately became official. "We couldn't give out that sort of information." Her face could, however, and did. No.

"How about criminal docketings?"

"Why didn't you say so?" she demanded with considerable asperity. She extended a jiggly-fleshed arm, the sort seen so often on farm wives at summer church socials in the Midwest. "Across the hall, at Traffic."

Kearny thanked her, but she had already returned to the gossip. Across the hall was a set of double windows and a counter. Two Mexican women, one holding a very loud baby, were paying a traffic fine; they laid their dollar bills down on the counter separately, as if each were made of fine Spanish lace. A hard-faced man in khaki, with a black eye, was losing an argument about a warrant for unpaid moving violations with an equally hard-faced deputy.

Kearny's deputy obviously was just waiting out his pension, which meant he was cooperative, good-natured, unhurried, efficient.

"Griffin, Charles M. Docketed to Judge Bailey Johnson's court at nine-thirty A.M. on Tuesday, June thirteenth. Drunk driving, violation of the right-of-way."

"You know the case personally?" asked Kearny in apparent idleness.

"He jumped bail back in February. Gerald Coogan Bail Bonds, 913 Main Street, Martinez, had to forfeit six bills bail. This clown's been in three HBD accidents since he bought that T-Bird last October. When they finally get him in front of the judge, he'll lose his license, period-the-end. Johnson had a daughter put in the hospital a few years ago by a drunk driver, he *loves* to see those babies turn up in his court."

Ballard hadn't been here, either. Kearny paused before getting into the Ford wagon. Three had-been-drinking accidents in five months. That California Street landlady could be right; he *could* be in jail, probably the county jug over in Martinez. Ballard, with the Wanda Moher lead he'd gotten from the police, but without the bail-bond lead obtained by Kearny here, would first check Wanda and any leads developed from her before hitting Martinez.

So Kearny would check on the jail and the bail bondsman first.

Martinez was an old town, almost a company town, created and sustained as a deepwater port for tankers coming up from the Bay to off-load their cargoes of crude at the Shell Oil Cracking Plant. The plant itself looked like a science-fiction city: great vertical towers and stacks, tall and lean and industrial against the round-topped hills beyond which lay Carquinez Straits. When Kearny entered town on one-way Howard Street, he could smell the dark, intense reek of oil through the open window. Not so distasteful when your job depended on it. The old story. Bucks.

The Contra Costa county jail was right across the street from the new twelve-story administration building, carefully decorated with palmetto palms, which was remarkably out of phase with the old sleepy town. The jail was the sort they had built when the town had been young: covering a whole city block, satisfyingly squat, dark, and of ugly, gray stone. The windows were narrow barred slits.

Kearny went up concrete steps, through open battered metal doors painted to resemble wood, to stop at the heavily barred cage. Signs fixed to the mesh laid out visiting hours, the fact that all guns had to be checked at the desk, the fact that ex-cons could not visit until six months after their release, and that ex-felons could not visit at all.

"What can I do for you?"

He was an athletic-looking young deputy with a large soup-strainer mustache. Kearny asked if Charles M. Griffin was a guest there, receiving hospitality for his tax dollars. He was not. On the way out, Kearny passed another deputy, hard but not hard-faced, bringing in a handcuffed prisoner with red-rimmed eyes, the twitches, and the sniffles. Coming down off a high, off the white horse, off the big H, down to brutal reality: a six-by-eight cell and screaming cold turkey until he admitted habituation and was transferred to a hospital wing.

Kearny U-turned back to Main, found a metered space in front of Snooks Jewelers, walked back to 913. It was on the main drag of a business district still flavored with small-town America. A few blocks away, Main deadended in a large green wooded hill rising up against paleblue California sky. Gerald Coogan Bail Bonds was a narrow stone-fronted building with dark-green verticalslat blinds.

Behind a counter inside was a desk with three telephones and a gray-haired woman with thick ankles. The lower half of her face said Grandma; Kearny could have cut himself on what the upper half said.

"Is Mr. Coogan in?"

She made a gesture toward the partition behind the desk which hid the enclosed interview cubicles. "With a client. I'm Missus."

"That's fine." Kearny laid his card on the counter, the card with *investigations, thefts, embezzlements, repossessions, skip-tracing, collections* blocked in the upper lefthand corner, *licensed and bonded, state and city, nationwide affiliates* in the upper right. He said, "We're trying to get a line on an ex-client of yours named Charles M. Griffin."

She made a two-word comment about Griffin and his mother that was probably more ritual than fact, then added, "Hell, we've had a warrant out on him since February; he burned us for six bills."

Kearny shook his head in bogus commiseration. Bail bondsmen usually got more than adequate security; one

of them getting burned was like a cat sitting twice on a
hot stove burner. It just hardly ever happened. He liked it.

"How'd he get into you for the cash?"

"He knew—" she stopped abruptly, then shrugged very
casually. "Favor for a friend—you know."

"What about his lawyer? Can't he help you?"

"Hawkley? Hell, he's . . ." She stopped again. "Hell, he
probably knows less about Griffin than we do."

Which Kearny doubted. Lawyers *always* knew more
about their clients than anyone else, and an old-line bail
bondsman like Ma Coogan would know that very well.
Something was a bit out of focus in the relationships
here, which made him ask for Hawkley's address. This
was rewarded with another appreciable pause before she
figured out there was no casual way she could refuse.

"Wayne Hawkley, 1942 Colfax Street. In Concord."

On the way back to Concord he tried, again unsuccess-
fully, to raise Ballard. He was looking forward to Wayne
Hawkley, who was almost surely the friend the Coogans
had been doing a favor for when they had gone bail for
Griffin without any collateral.

Kearny was waiting at the angle-intersection where
Concord Avenue became Galindo Street, behind a truck
trailer making a left-hand turn, when Ballard turned right
into Mount Diablo Street off Willow Pass Road a block
away. The truck blocked Kearny's vision; when the light
changed he followed its left turn into Willow Pass. He
didn't look down Mount Diablo Street when he passed
the intersection, because he was checking street signs for
Colfax Street, so he didn't see Ballard's car. If he had,
they would have teamed up, might never have caught up
with Charles M. Griffin, might never have laid the blocks
to the murderer who had struck down Bart Heslip. It
was that close.

The law offices of Wayne E. Hawkley, 1942 Colfax
Street, were in a one-story cinder block building with
red-brick fronting, plate-glass windows with the inevitable
aluminum frames, and tan drapes drawn against the sun.

Kearny parked across the street at 2:12 P.M. Inside, a

Spanish-American and a Caucasian waited patiently for attention. Neither looked prosperous, but the office looked prosperous enough to make up for it. There was an immense, bare, very expensive hardwood desk, empty, and a smaller, more functional secretary's desk set at right angles to it behind a partition. Kearny put one of his plain cards on the secretary's desk.

"Mr. Hawkley is busy, sir. And these other gentlemen—"

"I'll wait."

"If I could have some idea what it is concerning, sir . . ."

"I'll wait," said Kearny again, wondering, by the secretary's manner, whether he should have genuflected upon entering.

The secretary was lean and dark and intense-looking, wearing a dark-brown blouse and a beige jumper that showed a lot of slender leg. There was a hint of bafflement and irritation behind her rimless glasses. "Whatever you wish, sir."

It was twenty minutes before she paused at the head of the passageway behind the big empty desk with Kearny's business card in her hand. "That way, sir." The distaste in her voice was unmistakable.

She led him into a strictly functional air-conditioned office where an early-thirties type in shirt sleeves was reading a brief. He was one of the "new lawyers" so popularized by television: hirsute, goateed, wearing a loud striped shirt and a wide tie like a slice of pizza— concerned, involved, idealistic, shallow and glib.

He looked up with carefully calculated irritation. "What is it, Madeline? I told you I was too busy—"

"This is a Mr. Kearny. He insisted—"

"Yes, Dan Kearny," said Kearny heartily. "Mr. Hawkley?"

"I'm Norbert Franks, Mr. Hawkley's assistant. I screen—"

"Uh-uh," said Kearny.

"Huh?"

People didn't talk to him that way. People, Kearny had an idea, didn't even talk to Madeline that way. "Pull up the lower jaw before you drool on that pretty tie, sonny." He turned back to the girl, his voice thick and heavy. "Let's quit playing around and have Hawkley out here."

"Private eye. Big deal," sneered Franks. "A dime a dozen . . ."

Kearny turned back to him. The voice trailed off under that icy gray gaze; finally his hand began fidgeting with the slice of pizza and his eyes dropped to the brief. It wasn't his day. The girl started off with angry strides. So silently that she didn't know he was there until she had opened the next door down the hall, Kearny fell in right behind her.

"Thanks, honey," he said, sliding by her into the room.

She yelped in dismay. A stooped, very tall man in a three-hundred-dollar gray-blue pinstripe was just biting the end from a cigar. His battered old hardwood rolltop dated from the turn of the century, as did he. Clear blue eyes, much younger than the face, came up to meet Kearny's gray ones through old-fashioned spectacles and the first wreath of fragrant smoke. There was no surprise in the eyes. His thin hair was black enough to be dyed but probably wasn't.

"Mr. Kearny, sir. A pleasure, believe me."

His hand was rough and gnarled, as if he had chopped a lot of cordwood in his day. Kearny sat down across the desk from him. "You must shove one hell of a lot of bail-bond clients their way."

A glint appeared in the blue eyes. Kearny could almost see the mind behind them working it through. Almost. Hawkley had a thin, lined face that probably hadn't given anything away since 1927, the year a framed certificate on the wall said he had passed the California State Bar.

"That boy Norbert has a big mouth on him, ain't he?" The ain't would once have been deliberate, something for the juries that had become habitual.

"And a lousy bedside manner. If he's your son learning the business, buy him a shoestore."

The old man chuckled, opened a lower desk drawer while waving away the secretary still standing in the doorway. "Shut it behind you, Maddy."

She shot a look of pure hatred at Kearny, tried to slam the door peevishly behind her, only to have it yanked right out of her hand by the pneumatic closer. "God-*damn!*" she said in a positively venomous voice.

Hawkley had produced from a drawer a bottle of Wild Turkey and a pair of shot glasses. Kearny said, "I'll give her two hundred a month more than she gets here."

"Wouldn't be worth it to her, not with the commute. She likes a tennis lunch." Pride entered his voice. "She's my granddaughter."

"Congratulations."

"Norbert's my sister's boy. Plumb awful, ain't he? Wants to be one of these new poverty lawyers, I figger he's going to make it the hard way. Cheers."

The Wild Turkey went down neat; bourbon like that needed no chaser, not even any comment. Hawkley sighed and capped the bottle.

"Charles M. Griffin. What do you want to know about him?"

Kearny considered for a moment. Coogan, the bail bondsman, had phoned up Hawkley that a private investigator was on the way. And Hawkley had tried to give him the run-around. Why? Something to do with Griffin? Doubtful.

"His current address."

"Can't help you," said Hawkley promptly.

"He probably assaulted one of our men with intent to commit murder on Wednesday A.M.," said Kearny. "The police read it as an accident and we haven't tried to make them think any different. Yet."

Hawkley was watching him thoughtfully. "Meaning?"

"I'm personally taking this wherever I have to take it."

"You're big?" said Hawkley abruptly.

"Big enough. Fifteen field agents out of San Francisco and Oakland covering the city, the Peninsula, East Bay and Marin. Nine branch offices from Eureka to Long

Beach. Three others in the corporations fully licensed besides myself."

He added the last deliberately; three other valid licenses meant that anyone with enough clout in Sacramento to get Kearny's pulled still wouldn't stop DKA from operating.

Hawkley cleared his throat; the message had gotten through. "Chuck Griffin is *all* you're after?"

"No wooden horses," Kearny assured him.

"Damn!" exclaimed the old man regretfully. "I *still* can't help you, and I ain't sure you'll believe that. Chuck Griffin's daddy was one of my first clients back in '27. An improvident man, died broke in a car wreck in '53. Or was it '54? I felt bad when Chuck burned Coogan on that bail money, after I sort of rammed him down their throats as a client." He laughed dryly. "Not *too* bad, of course." He depressed a button on his squawk box. "Maddy, get me that Mount Diablo Street address on Griffin."

Kearny felt a flicker of excitement; the DKA file showed no Mount Diablo Street address.

Madeline's rather snotty tones came on. "That's 1377, Mr. Hawkley. On a letter returned to us as *unknown this address* on March thirteenth this year."

"That's all I've got, Mr. Kearny. Our letter to Chuck was forwarded from the California Street address, finally came back here. I ain't heard from Chuck since February. I sent Norbert out to Mount Diablo Street, they'd never heard of Chuck. 'Course, Norbert . . ."

"Yeah." Kearny stood up. A hell of an intriguing old scoundrel, but he was a riddle Kearny didn't have to solve. "A pleasure to do business with you, sir."

"And with you." Hawkley also stood. He was a good six-three; he probably didn't weigh any more than the detective's compact 170. "I trust my Wild Turkey wasn't wasted."

"I'm a pro, Hawkley. I only get curious when I'm paid to."

"Would there were more of us in this sinful world," sighed the old lawyer piously.

Sixteen

Excitement constricted Ballard's chest. Parked on the crumbling, weed-covered concrete drive at 1377 Mount Diablo Street was a red car with a white convertible top and . . . Hell. Convertible. A dusty red Oldsmobile compact, not a T-Bird.

He turned in midblock, came back to park across the street. Beyond him was a great open scar where the houses had been razed and the earth scooped out for Bay Area Rapid Transit. In this minor moon crater were stacks of cement-reinforcing rod, coils of hose, stakes with yellow tags on them, parked trucks. The air was filled with dust, the staccato slap of diesel motors. Bulldozers and earth-movers crawled clumsily about like blind beetles seeking a way out.

The white-plaster house was small, L-shaped, one-story, with the pale-pink numbers 1-3-7-7 set in descending order down one of the four-by-four porch posts. Old, crummy, poorly kept-up. He was tense. The trail might lie here, despite the insurance agent's belief that it was a dead address, and he might miss it.

He crossed the street under the shade of the thriving front-yard maple. Running along the left side of the property was an overgrown hedge; Ballard went down the narrow space between it and the side of the garage to cup his eyes and peer in a dusty cobwebbed window. An earth floor overflowed with meaningless debris, including an old brass bedstead, a ripped mattress, treadless car tires, three ruined tricycles.

He walked back, stood by the Olds to listen to the pop of diesels. In the front yard, knee-deep in weeds, were two big recently rained-on cardboard boxes of trash. The front porch was strewn with a miniature obstacle course of broken toys. Growing up across the front steps, when he waded over there, was a flourishing sweet-pea vine.

He rang the bell.

After a few moments a woman opened the door, giving him a momentary glimpse of a cluttered living room, a new color TV spewing afternoon bathos, a new round felt-topped table suitable for poker.

"If you're selling someth—"

"Buying," said Ballard.

That stopped her. She was in shorts and halter, barefoot, with her face carefully made-up and brilliant toenails and fingernails. The halter revealed deep cleavage between full breasts; her legs were good, the bare belly between shorts and halter flat and hard. Her face was narrow and vixenish under gleaming brown hair.

"*What* are you buying?"

"Information about Griff." No flicker in her wide brown eyes at the nickname. Hell. "Charles M. Griffin. I heard he's staying here."

She shook an almost regretful head. "Man, you heard wrong. I don't know him."

"How about your husband?"

She shifted her weight to throw out one hip in a deliberately sensuous pose. Her thigh brushed the back of Ballard's hand. He drew the hand back quickly; she was trouble looking for a place to happen, and he didn't want it to happen to him.

"I s'pose. If he knew him at work, like."

"Maybe Griff is one of the poker players."

"Poker?" She turned her head to follow his gaze to the table. "Oh. Poker." She added quickly, "No. Never heard of a Griffin."

Ballard gestured at the Olds compact, put a smile on his face. "When I drove up, I thought that was Griff's car. He was driving a red and white T-Bird hardtop last time I saw him."

She frowned, then exclaimed suddenly, "Wait a minute, *that* rings a bell. Red and white T-Bird hardtop. Loaded, power-everything, all the goodies—air, power windows, seats, steering, brakes. Sure. Howie Odum has been driving a car like that for a month or so. I had a ride in it last week . . ." She bit it off, like a child realizing it has just told a secret.

Last week! If Griffin's car had been around then, Griffin himself must also have been close by.

"Where could I find Mr. Odum?"

Instead of answering, she said, "Griffin. Charles Griffin. That's the name. Howie told me back in April, couple of weeks after he got the car, there might be some mail coming for that name, I should just hold it. He said he'd pick it up every now and then. But didn't any come—unless my husband, he found it in the box and marked it unknown or something."

From inside came the tentative, just-waking wail of a child. She looked at Ballard with a shocked, almost furtive expression. "Hey, man, you won't be coming around here again, will you?"

"Not if I find Griffin."

"For God's sake, don't say anything to my husband about Howie." She put a hand on his forearm. "Please? He'd just kill me if he knew that Howie had been around. He . . . they aren't friends any more."

"I have to know Odum's address," said Ballard ruthlessly.

"Look, I don't *have* it. Honest. I mean, there wasn't anything *wrong*, me riding around with him in the T-Bird, we didn't . . . *you* know." Which probably meant they had. The kid squalled again in the background. "But I left the baby here alone and all, the other two were in school . . ."

"What bars does Odum hang around?"

"He doesn't. He's on . . . look, he got into trouble. With the Feds. He . . . you see, a couple, three years ago he got into a bind and well, he . . . forged some checks, including some of Bob's. So you know, Bob and him don't . . ."

"Odum's trouble was connected with these forged checks?"

"Ah, look, I got to change the kid. I've leveled with you, you won't get me in trouble with Bob, will you?"

"Of course not," he said soothingly, "Mrs.—"

"Sharon Beag . . . ah, Sharon."

He didn't push. Names were easy to learn. Besides, he'd gotten all there was to get here. Odum would have been sentenced in Concord, if he'd been paper-hanging in local bars. He realized that she had started to shut the door, gave it one more try.

"You must have *some* idea where Odum's living."

Her eyes were made beady by peering through the narrow opening. "Maybe down around Oakland, Alameda, like that. He never really said . . . honest . . ."

The door was shut. Ballard went down the steps to flounder out across the rankly overgrown yard. He stumbled over a hidden wheelless coaster wagon and almost went down, cursing, expecting to flush a covey of quail.

In his mind, as he got into the car, two images suddenly came together. Sharon, bored mother of three who had kept her looks despite the babies, getting into the back seat of the T-Bird with Howie Odum, just-released convict. And Cheri over on California Street not a mile away, wrestling with Griffin's kinky friend with a flashlight. Easy to see both men as the same man. Howie Odum. A writer of bad checks, which meant a con man, which meant plausible, smooth. And maybe tall and handsome. And just out of stir, perhaps sexually maladjusted because of it . . .

Odum, sure as hell mixed up with Griffin, driving his car.

Odum was the key.

Ballard pulled from the curb. The radio gave its usual warm-up *squeergk,* like water going down a drain, and then said to him in a very loud and clear Dan Kearny voice, "SF-1 calling SF-6. Come in, Ballard."

He scrabbled at the clipped mike. That voice was much too strong and ungarbled to have come from Oakland Control on the other side of the hills.

"This is SF-6," he said.

"I'll meet you in that little coffee shop on Willow Pass and Mount Diablo Street in three minutes, over."

"Don't eat anything there," said Ballard. "Their food is lousy."

"10-4. SF-1 over and out."

He struck the steering wheel happily with the heel of his hand. Dan Kearny was in the field! Kearny would have some ideas about finding Howard Odum. And through him, Charles M. Griffin. The jaws were closing. Then, as he pulled up beside Kearny's Ford wagon in front of the coffee shop, he wondered: Now, how in hell did Kearny find out that I was on Mount Diablo Street?

"From the attorney, Hawkley," said Kearny.

He added nothing about the odd can of worms he had opened in the Hawkley/Coogan relationship. They had been kicking around the case for forty minutes.

"Anyway, there's nothing more to get at that address," said Ballard. "I squeezed her dry. Since it was a Federal rap—"

"That I doubt," said Kearny. Even more, he doubted that Ballard had squeezed Sharon dry. Larry just wasn't that good with women. The best way was to push them fast and hard to where they started crying but before they got stubborn. It was an art. He went on, "The Feds come in only on interstate—Odum was probably just kiting checks in local bars and somebody blew the whistle. He was probably in Quentin, not Lompoc."

"So how do we find out?" asked Ballard.

"We go see his parole officer. If he was sent up two years ago and is out now, he's out on parole." He looked at his watch. "Three-thirty, plenty of time for you to get down to Parole and Community Services Division in Oakland. It's on Grove just off West Grand. And remember: you're a repo man looking for a car you think Odum is driving."

"Nothing about Bart getting whacked on the head or—"

"Absolutely not." Kearny made a face. "Even the

coffee is lousy here. A pure and simple repossession. Your lever is the fact that guys on parole are supposed to get prior permission from their PO before they even *drive* a motor vehicle, because of insurance problems. Come at him right, the PO ought to come up with Odum's address." He paused a second. "Anything strike you as interesting about this Odum character?"

"I was wondering if he could be the kinky cat who was trying to play games with Cheri in February—just before Griffin took off."

"Or was taken off," said Kearny. Ballard stopped dead in the act of snapping shut his attaché case. "February," said Kearny. "It all happened in February. Better find out whether Odum had been released on parole before February eighth, the night Cheri had her bout with the flashlight kink."

"What did you mean about Griffin maybe being *taken* off?"

"Look it over. *No*body's seen him, that we've talked to, since February ninth."

"He called Cheri in March," Ballard pointed out.

"If she's telling the truth, *somebody* called her. From a phone in a bar, sounding drunk, with music being played loudly in the background. So loudly that she says she had trouble understanding him."

Ballard felt . . . *cheated*. As if somebody had taken his case and turned it upside down. He had been concentrating on Griffin so hard that if it turned out he wasn't it after all . . .

"He sold off his furniture, rented the place in San Jose . . ."

"Neither of which makes sense, not for Griffin. A *newspaper ad* sold the furniture—and the buyers were instructed to pay Cheri with checks she couldn't cash. The Midfield Road house was rented by *phone,* with a cashier's check deposit against the rent which was *mailed* in."

"He identified himself to the bank as Griffin—"

"Only verbally. Nobody checks ID when you buy a cashier's check, why should they? You're paying for it in cash. Which brings us right back to our ex-con, Howard

Odum. He *seems* to be driving Griffin's car; we *know* he's diverting Griffin's mail."

Ballard thought about it for a while. Finally he said, "If Griffin wasn't an embezzler, then why should Odum—"

"I didn't say he wasn't an embezzler. What was that figure Elkin gave you? Thirty thousand bucks might be missing? Let's assume for a second that it is; what does Griffin do with it? Bank it? No way. Safe-deposit box? Risky. Probably bury it in the back yard in a bunch of fruit jars or something. In the middle of this, his old lady dies. He's cut free, he starts buying, spending, boozing. Boozing heavy, according to the Concord cops—three HBD accidents in three months. He gets drunk one night with an ex-con named Odum, a hard-nose, maybe, just out of stir with a hard-on against humanity, lets something drop . . . You can take it from there."

Ballard looked at his watch, stood up. "Four o'clock. I have to get going. Did you check with Giselle about how Bart is?"

"No change as of two hours ago. Call me as soon as you get back on this side of the hills. And if you *do* get an address on Odum, *don't go up against him alone.* You got that?"

"Loud and clear," said Ballard. He meant it. He didn't want some son of a bitch putting *him* over a cliff. Not even in a Jaguar.

In the late afternoon wind, the plastic streamers over the tired old iron on the used-car lot whipped and danced. The place looked like an antique auto show. Ballard made his left turn from West Grand into Grove. It was 2229, an old tan-brick building, three stories, which stood alone among the razed weedy redevelopment lots.

"Let's try the unit supervisor first," suggested the switchboard operator behind the window inside the front door. She was a motherly sort, perhaps chosen for that quality. After working several keys and punching in and out of half a dozen sockets, she said, "Down the corridor to the right, far as it goes, then turn left and it will be the first door on the right at the bottom of the stairs. Mr. Savidge."

The halls were big, friendly, creaking, painted an institutional pale yellow. The offices were high-ceilinged; the Venetian blinds badly needed restringing. He wondered if the atmosphere was deliberate or had just happened; it probably was soothing to just-paroled convicts.

Mr. Saul Savidge was waiting at the door of his office with a handshake and a grin; a vaguely pear-shaped black man who confounded current terminology by being decidedly brown. He had a narrow mustache and short straightened hair combed back so severely that it made his head look too small for his face.

"Better take the straight-back instead of that swivel," he warned. "The shower upstairs leaks on the swivel."

Shower? Then he remembered the sign by the front entrance about the Crittendon Home, a halfway house for cons. He took the uncomfortable straight-backed chair closest to the battered wooden desk. On the wall was a printed sign, WARNING—THIS ROOM IS OCCUPIED BY A SEX MANIAC, and a tapestry sampler of Martin Luther King succoring a black man in shackles.

"I'm lucky to be assistant unit supervisor," said Savidge. "It gives me a one-man office. Tough to get a parolee to tell you his troubles when the cat at the next desk is hauling some poor bastard out in chains for parole violations."

Ballard explained what he wanted.

Savidge nodded thoughtfully. "Howie hasn't registered that T-Bird with me and he hasn't asked permission to drive it. How long has he had it, do you know?"

Ballard saw his opening. "How long has he been out?"

"Just after the first of the year . . ." He consulted a file. "Uh-huh. January fifth."

"This was just last week," said Ballard quickly. "Our informant, who knew Odum before his arrest and knew he was out, saw someone in our T-Bird he *thought* was Odum. It might not have been him."

Savidge nodded again, again thoughtfully. There was a disconcerting steel beneath the affable exterior that reminded Ballard that he was, after all, dealing with a law officer and not a social worker.

"All right, Mr. Ballard, I'm going to cooperate with you on this even though, as I'm sure you know, I'm under no legal compulsion to give you any information whatsoever."

"I realize that, sir."

"I'm cooperating because there is a possible parole violation involved here, and because *if* there is, it belongs in Odum's file. I carry a case load of seventy-five men, it's hell just trying to keep up with what each one is doing." He got a rueful look on his face. "The rules say they must 'maintain gainful employment'—so what do you find for a sixty-five-year-old man with an eighty-five IQ who's only good at exposing himself to little girls?"

Ballard didn't try to answer. He was there only for Odum's address. He got it.

"1684 Galindo Street, Concord. That's a rooming house run by the widow of an ex-con, actually. Odum has room four."

Ballard stood up and stuck out his hand. "You'll hear from me about Odum in a day or two."

"I'll appreciate that."

Outside, Ballard stopped under one of the sidewalk elms, drew a deep breath. He was damned happy he wasn't an ex-con on parole.

And pretty soon, they'd make Odum damned *un*happy that he was.

Seventeen

After Ballard left to interview the parole officer, Kearny called Oakland Control and had one of the girls look up 1377 Mount Diablo Street in the cross-directory. The entry read: *Beaghler, Robert, wife, Sharon, occupation: auto mechanic;* which checked with what Ballard had learned from Sharon, that her husband was named Bob and that the last name began with B-e-a-g. If the directory hadn't come through, he still would have had the utilities companies, garbage collection, voter registration records, real estate plot registrations, the postman—and, if you didn't care whether word got back to the subject, the neighbors.

While Ballard fought the freeway traffic to Oakland, Kearny sat on a quiet side street in Concord with the windows open and let his mind play with the case. There was still something bugging him about their new reconstruction with Odum as the villain. It was the sort of feeling that made you suddenly turn around and go back up to the house you had just left, and ask that one more question which broke the case.

For one thing, why would Odum, posing as Griffin, sell that furniture? Spite? And if *not* Odum, why would Griffin? He sure as hell didn't need the money. And, having sold it, why would he ask Cheri to send the checks to a San Jose address he had gone to great lengths up to that time to keep secret? That had been in March. In April, Odum had turned up with the car. Any connection?

Almost 5:30, where was Ballard? He couldn't go lean on Sharon yet: he wanted Beaghler home for that. She had been lying to Ballard, of course; she would have an address on Odum, it would not be the one the parole officer had. If Odum *was* their boy, he'd have a bolt-hole, a place the Adult Authority didn't know about. Too easy for the PO to make an unannounced visit, because when you were on parole, your legal residence was still a prison cell. And prison cells could be searched, any time, without any warrant or forewarning.

And if you happened to be sitting on thirty thousand bucks, say, you really wouldn't want the parole officer dropping by, would you? Especially not if you had killed someone to get that money.

Still, pegging Odum for it was just a hunch, nothing more. And look at some of the sour horses he had backed on hunches, down through the years. And after his lecture to Ballard about facts . . .

The radio sputtered, lapsed into silence, then Ballard's voice came through, choppy and distant.

". . . residence address . . . 10-4?"

"Repeat that address, over."

There was a blast of static, then Ballard's voice came on clear and thin, as if he were yelling down from a third-floor window. "1-6-8-4 Galindo Street . . . Concord . . ."

"All right, I'll meet you there. Outside, across the street . . ."

The rider's door opened and Kearny slid in. Ballard was parked across still-busy Galindo and down the block from 1684, a rambling old California residence which would have been built when the street was a country dirt road. Since World War II it had been encapsulated by a growing Concord; now it was a rooming house, soon it would be razed as standing on property too valuable for it.

"Any activity?" asked Ballard. He had seen Kearny's parked car when he had circled the block.

"A number of guys in and out, all men. Any of them could have been Odum, seeing that we don't know what he looks like." He glanced at Ballard. "The parole officer didn't have his picture?"

"I didn't ask." Ballard's voice just missed being defensive. It had been a long, hot, frustrating day, although the sun was low now, the air was cooling, neon signs were winking on. "I was supposed to be interested in a car, remember?"

"Just asking," said Kearny cheerfully. "I checked all the street parking, and got a look in the garage out behind the house. Nothing. The garage used to be a stables back when. I also went up to check on Odum's room."

He stopped there. Ballard figeted, finally asked, "And?"

"Locked. With a note on the door that Denny is over at Mary's."

"Whoever the hell they are," grumbled Ballard.

Kearny opened his door. "Let's go find out."

As they started up the walk to the old stately frame building, a man brushed past them. Odum? Ballard turned to look down the walk at the retreating back with a returning sense of frustration. Dammit, this place *had* to give them a lead to Griffin or, if Kearny was right, the man who had killed him and then had attacked Bart.

Had to; they didn't have any other leads left. And fewer than eight of their original seventy-two hours left.

Bart. Was he still lying there, unmoving? Unthinking? With his brain gouged by a depressed hunk of bone so he would always lie there, unmoving, unthinking?

There was no answer at the heavy hardwood door with the cheap metal 4 screwed to the panel. The note about Denny and Mary was still there.

"So now what?" asked Ballard in a voice heavy with fatigue. Kearny looked as fatigued as a diesel engine. Never missed a trick, the bastard, and never missed letting you know that he was taking it, either.

"Now we go talk to the landlady," he said. "Naturally."

The trouble with people was that they continually refused to fit into their neat little categories. Widow of a con, ran a rooming house full of ex-cons. If she was old, granny with a steel hatpin up her sleeve, right? If she was young, blowzy and full-blown, with meaty knees and the wrong color lipstick, right?

Wrong.

She was at first glance young, and she was close to chimerical—if Ballard had known the word. *Dreamlike* came to his mind when she opened the door. He didn't recognize the music this let out into the hall, but it was also rarefied, classical, all strings and violins, and so forth. By the lines in her face she was obviously well past forty, yet the face had an almost luminous serenity that was ageless. Even Kearny, Ballard noticed, was affected. His right hand actually started a motion as if he were going to take off the hat he wasn't wearing and almost never did.

"Good evening, gentlemen. Can I help you?"

The voice suggested that helping people was her only role in life. Kearny's voice was an obsequious rumble, like sounds from a bowling alley heard in the street outside.

"We're . . . terribly sorry to bother you, ma'am. We're trying to get in touch with the tenant in room four."

"Howie. Oh, I hope . . . He *isn't* in trouble?" Her eyes pleaded with this oddly assorted pair of hard-faced men.

Kearny should have answered, soothingly, that they were friends of good old Howie, and were interested in buying that new T-Bird he had. Instead, Kearny was affected enough to say, "We certainly hope not also, ma'am."

Ballard realized whom she reminded him of: Billie Burke in *The Wizard of Oz*. The good witch of whatever direction she was from. North?

Kearny said, "Do you know anyone named Denny, ma'am? Or Mary?"

"*I'm* Mary." Her eyes widened. "Oh dear, is that note still on Howie's door? Denny put that there on—goodness, that must have been on Tuesday evening . . ."

Tuesday evening? It was fitting together. It was all fitting.

"And you haven't seen Mr. Odum since then?"

"He *is* in trouble," she said sorrowfully.

Kearny's voice was almost glutinous. "I'm afraid he probably is. Would you know if Mr. Odum is . . . um . . . seeing a young lady?"

Ballard barely stifled a snort of self-disgust. He should

have thought of that himself. A charming, good-looking conman just out of Quentin wasn't going to remain celibate very long—as proved by Sharon; but he wasn't going to confine himself to a risky, hit-and-miss liaison with a married woman, either. Still, he was glad it was Kearny asking questions. He was glad he didn't have to hurt this gentle being who had created a quiet warm little world for herself and her charges.

Mary bobbed her head on its slender white swanlike neck. "Well, yes, I believe Howie *does* have a young lady with whom he can . . . well, you know, talk and things . . ." She trailed off, then added sorrowfully, "It must get so lonesome for those poor boys there in prison, without anyone of the opposite sex to make them *want* to act like gentlemen . . ."

"Yes, ma'am," said Kearny. Ballard hated the unction in his voice, necessary as it was to get Odum's whereabouts out of this sweet and gentle lady. "Now, if we could just have the young lady's name . . ."

Mary looked at them, her features placid. Finally she answered. "Piss off," she said distinctly. Distinctly, but also gently.

Kearny was still laughing when they got back into Ballard's car. Ballard was stiff with rage.

"When she dies," said Kearny, "I'd like to mount her and hang her on the wall at DKA. Just as a reminder."

"Over a sign reading *Cheer Up, She Might Still Be Alive,*" snarled Ballard.

Dammit, there was nothing to laugh about. There went their last lead down the drain. They didn't have a thing. Not a *thing*.

"I'll go over to Beaghler's place for one last check," said Kearny cheerfully. "You stake out this place in case the T-Bird shows."

It wouldn't, of course, thought Ballard; they both knew that. He burst out, "What gets me, Dan, is that goddamn woman covering up for Odum with his parole officer! Hell, I'll bet she's got hot goods in the garage from jobs her tenants have pulled with her furnishing the alibi."

"Probably," said Kearny with a grin. He started to get out.

" 'Why, it *couldn't* have been little Howie, Mr. Parole Officer,' " said Ballard mincingly. " 'Howie was drinking tea and eating crumpets with me at the exact *instant* that . . .' Oh, *shit!*"

Eighteen

At exactly 7:07 P.M., a black hand jerked convulsively on the white sheet. Corinne Jones' head snapped up, her mouth popped open in excitement and disbelief. It had been sixty-six hours.

Heslip sighed, stirred, tried to roll over. Corinne was already clawing the bell at the head of the bed which was to bring the nurse. It did, fast. And the doctor.

Heslip moaned, made a sort of clucking sound in his throat, and began a regular even grating sound. The little mod medic, Whitaker, far from being alarmed at the sound, seemed delighted. He laid a hand on Corinne's arm in a gesture that should have been avuncular but which somehow came off closer to a caress. He chuckled softly.

Bart Heslip had started to snore.

At exactly 7:07 P.M., Dan Kearny drove down Mount Diablo Street in Concord. The sun had another hour of Daylight Saving, but it was low and its light was pink-tinged. The shadows it now cast were long and thin, unlike the round fat ones Ballard had found earlier.

Kearny went a full block beyond the house before U-turning, and parked far enough down the street so his car would be out of sight. He ambled slowly back, tasting the neighborhood. Small one-stories built as veterans' dream homes after World War II. Still bungalows then, instead of the pervasive California ranch style.

In front of the house next door, Kearny paused to pat

a mongrel pup that had cantered up with unsuspicious puppy friendliness. Kearny's hard gray eyes roamed the street, the setup at the Beaghler house.

There were too many cars parked in front of it. Five of them.

The red and white Olds compact convertible in the driveway—Sharon's car, of course. A dusty black Chevy Nova with the slightly splay-footed stance that too-wide tires give small cars. Beaghler's. Probably jazzed-up to get out and move, a useful trait for a number of things both legal and illegal.

Kearny thumped the dog in the ribs. The dog loved it. Looking too hard for illegal setups today? No. There were those extra cars outside Beaghler's house. Three of them. And they were all wrong.

What about people over to supper? Ballard's description of the living room said no. Even crappy housekeepers clean up for company. But what about an early poker game with the boys? That was a possibility—what did men care about housekeeping as long as the beer held out? Yes, a good possibility. Except.

Except that Kearny knew damned near everything there was to know about cars. Not just how to open them without keys, or run them without switching on the ignition. Everything. And just driving by those three late-model sedans, all with California plates, all recently washed, he had spotted the odd fact about them.

All three were rental cars.

He gave the dog a final friendly thump, went by the cars toward the house. Check. Each had the unobtrusive Dymo-printed adhesive tab used to identify rental vehicles. Rear bumper. Lower left-hand corner of the windshield. Back of the rear-view mirror.

Which meant three *different* rental companies.

Picking his way across the overgrown yard, Kearny tried to come up with a legitimate explanation. Friends coming in from out of state. Then why the three different companies? Family reunion, people coming in at different times from different places. On a weekday? A business conference. That could explain the cars; coincidence could explain the choice of three different rent-a-car companies. It also could explain the poker table. A conference, not cards.

But how many business conferences with out-of-state associates did an auto mechanic living in a twenty-five-year-old $18,000 tract home have? *Legitimate* business conferences?

Kearny rang the bell.

He stood turned slightly from the door, the perfect picture of a bored salesman or house-to-houser. Then the door opened, and Kearny immediately recast his role.

This man had never been an auto mechanic, or a homeowner, or would have worked for anyone else. He was wide and blocky, with flat square shoulders, a good half-head taller than Kearny's five-nine. His hands were out of a foundry, his wrists roped with veins. His face was bony, as flat and hard as the shoulders, rough-hewn in the same foundry as the hands.

He didn't say anything, he didn't have to. He confirmed what the clustered rental cars suggested, and made it even more certain by stepping out on the porch and closing the door firmly behind him.

Kearny had to make the motions, anyway. "Mr. Beaghler?"

"No." Just a monosyllable, nothing more.

"How about the little lady of the house? Is Mrs. Beaghler—"

"No."

"You mean she isn't here at the present time, or that—"

"I already said no."

The big catlike man reached behind him without looking, twisted the knob, started to slide through the door sideways and back in, automatically not letting Kearny see into the house. As he automatically had stepped outside the door and shut it behind him, just in case Kearny had been fuzz. Once you let a cop in, he was in. If you came out to him and shut the door, then he needed a warrant to go through it.

Until Kearny spoke, he had no idea he was going to; the face was totally unfamiliar. But something in his computer mind, programed by a quarter-century of investigations to indelibly retain detail, because detail so often broke cases, had recognized those hands, the ears set flat to the square skull, the black dry hair, the voice. Even though it had been a single night ten years before.

"Parker," he said.

The door stopped closing. Eyes of flawed onyx regarded him thoughtfully. Kearny wished he had broken his own rule about carrying the S&W four-inch .41 Magnum for which he had a permit. The thoughts behind those eyes made a gun seem a comforting idea.

"What did you call me?"

"Parker."

"You're making a mistake," he said flatly. Whether the mistake was in the name or in using the name wasn't clear. "The name is Latham."

Kearny allowed himself a shrug. "It was Parker in 1962. You've gotten a new face since then, but the rest is the same."

Then he saw the recognition in the eyes, in the slight relaxation of the tough, muscle-roped body.

"My name's Kearny," he went on. "You were vagged in Bakersfield, broke out of the prison farm. A woman from Fresno gave you a ride, ended up taking you home with her for a two-day shack-up while the heat died down. You never told her you were the one they wanted, but she knew. She didn't care. She was my wife's sister. I stayed at the house the second night. We killed a bottle between us."

The big man came back out on the porch. His eyes were still watchful, but not at the moment murderous. "I was Ronald Casper then."

"She heard you telephoning a guy in Chicago, collect. He wouldn't accept a call from Casper, you had to use the name Parker. She told me about it afterwards, after you left. She still talks about you. I never told her she was just an easy way for you to be off the street for a couple of days."

Parker shrugged; he didn't seem to care about that. He said, "So what is it now?"

"I'm looking for a paroled con named Howard Odum."

The big man waited, perfectly still, perfectly relaxed, totally dangerous. Thoughts moved behind the stony eyes. He said, "Odum is a friend of Beaghler's?"

"Was. Friend of the wife's now. Beaghler doesn't know." Kearny added carefully, "This has nothing to do with anything Beaghler's into now."

Parker decided. He opened the door enough to stick his head in and call. "Sharon."

In a few moments the woman Ballard had described came out. She carelessly let the door swing wide enough to give Kearny a glimpse of at least three more men in the living room. The plunder squad. Parker shut the door again.

Ballard had been right about Sharon's obvious physical charms, but Parker looked at her like something for sale by the pound. "He wants Odum. Tell him."

"Odum?" Her voice was strident. "I haven't seen Howie since—"

Parker made an impatient movement with one hand. Her eyes tried to meet the onyx ones, couldn't.

She cleared her throat. "1684 Galindo Street."

The address Ballard had gotten from the parole officer. No good. Kearny wanted the rabbit's bolt-hole, not the main burrow. And she would know what it was. She'd have gotten it from Odum on the back seat of the T-Bird in some country lane while he was busy between her legs.

Parker looked over at Kearny queryingly. Kearny shook his head. He turned back to Sharon. "Try again."

It was impossible for her to look innocent, but she tried. "Honest," she said, "that's his address."

Parker didn't move, but the atmosphere changed. To Kearny it was as though the other man were leaning over her like an oncoming storm. You could almost see the shadow crossing her face. "Once more," Parker said, and there wasn't anything in his voice at all.

"Well, uh—" She licked her lips, gave Kearny a quick pleading look, as though somehow he might protect her from what was happening. Kearny kept his own face blank, and she looked back at Parker, saying, "Maybe he means, uh, Howie's girl friend over in Antioch."

Parker glanced at Kearny, and Kearny nodded. Parker looked back at Sharon, and waited.

Sharon had started to blink now, and once she started talking, the words poured out in a nervous stream: "He . . . stays over with her a lot. She . . . I don't know her name, but her address is . . . ah, 1-9-0-2- Gavallo Road. It's a like new apartment building, twelve units. Howie said—"

"Good," Parker said. "I'll be right in."

She'd been dismissed. It took her a second to get it, and then she scrambled back into the house like a cat leaving a full bathtub.

Parker turned to Kearny. "I'd hate to think you'd memorized those car plates to find out who rented them."

"What cars?" said Kearny.

The door closed behind him before he was even off the porch.

Some kind of heist, probably. Parker had the sort of cold, lawless control that went with that sort of planning. He'd watch the papers for the next few days for something big, local: a bank vault, an armored car, something like that. Or Parker might kill the whole deal because Kearny had recognized him. Parker wouldn't still be around if he weren't a very cautious man while being simultaneously a very bold one.

Getting into the car, Kearny realized that the back of his neck ached. When he rubbed it, his hand came away smeary with sweat. Tension. But what the hell, he had Odum's ass nailed to the wall. Thanks to Parker.

Nineteen

"You going to start the car?" asked Kearny mildly. He checked his watch. "Your seventy-two hours are almost up."

That was it. That was just it. Kearny bringing up the goddamn deadline *now*. The perfect psychological moment. Waste an hour on stakeout while Kearny is wasting an hour at the Beaghler house, then he comes back and gets into your car and calmly tells you to get going. Get going where?

With a muttered curse, Ballard started to open his door.

"What the hell do you think you're doing?" demanded Kearny.

"I'm going back inside and turn sweet little Mary upside down and shake her until an address falls out. That bitch knows where Odum is, Dan, and I'm—"

"So do we."

"I'm going to— Huh?" Ballard froze, stupidly, half in and half out of the car.

"1902 Gavallo Road, Antioch. We don't know the name of the girl Odum's shacking with, and we don't know the apartment number, but there's only twelve units in the building . . ."

Ballard had a sinking feeling. "How in *hell* did you get all that?"

"I turned a bitch upside down and shook her until an address fell out." Kearny added nothing about Parker. The big, hard criminal had played straight with him.

"Sharon?" Dammit, would he *ever* get so he didn't blindly believe whatever they wanted to tell him?

Kearny gave him a version of the interview with Sharon Beaghler sanitized of Parker as they headed east on California 4, out across the valley floor toward the Sacramento River delta and Antioch. Right out of reach of KDM 366 Control, on which Giselle would shortly be trying to call them.

Bart Heslip opened his eyes and looked at the ceiling. What in the hell went on? Where . . . He licked his lips. He turned his head from side to side. How . . .

"Christ," he said, "I'm thirsty. What time . . ."

His voice trailed off. Before anyone could tell him that it was a handful of seconds past 8:47 on the evening of Friday, May 12, and that he had been in coma for three days, he started snoring again.

Dr. Arnold Whitaker looked around at the exhausted Corinne Jones, the slat-thin red-headed nurse whose behind he had a passion for patting, the little Filipino aide who had just brought Corinne a glass of orange juice and who had recently been catching Whitaker's magnificently roaming eye. Whitaker beamed.

Corinne, laughing and crying at the same time, headed for a phone.

Their headlights splayed a little white world out in front of them which fled down the highway at their approach. It was still warm enough, in the cup protected by the dim round-topped hills, for them to have their windows open. The wind raked their hair like blowing leaves. Tension was building inside Ballard.

"Do you really think this is it, Dan?" he asked tightly.

"If it isn't, we've wasted the day."

Kearny drew on his cigarette, stubbed it in the ashtray. Ballard found his lips were dry. Howard Odum, murderer. He couldn't leave it alone.

"Ah . . . how do you plan to play it if he *is* there, Dan?"

"By ear," said Kearny.

A car on the other side of the highway divider poured a long stream of horn-noise against their windshield as it whipped by. Probably teen-agers, juiced up on the warmth of the night and the fact of their youth.

"Do we . . . ah, try to take him ourselves?"

Kearny's square face was without expression; the glare of another passing car momentarily touched his massive jaw. "We aren't cops, Larry; and we don't have enough evidence to give the cops. We don't have *any* evidence. Not about Griffin, not about Odum, not even about Bart being attacked."

"Then what—"

"We're private investigators on a routine repossession assignment, remember? Running down a 1972 Thunderbird two-door hardtop for our clients, California Citizens Bank. When we find the car we will take possession of it on their behalf." He paused to light another cigarette, and shook one from the pack for Ballard. "But I'm betting that Odum will have to do *something* about us when we take the car away from him. Whatever he was willing to kill for last February, or last Tuesday, sure as hell hasn't gone away."

Meaning they were deliberately trying to provoke some sort of action by Odum. Action, for instance, like the attack on Bart. Well, Ballard thought, fair enough. There were two of them. Then another, oddly disturbing thought struck him. "What if he *doesn't* try to stop us, Dan?"

"Then we wait. We wait for Bart to wake up and point the finger at him. And while we're waiting, he won't un-zip his pants in a men's room without somebody putting it in a DKA report. Twenty-four hours around-the-clock overt surveillance if necessary."

His voice was surprisingly rough, full of a suppressed fury that Ballard found totally unexpected. Dan Kearny *involved* in a case? *Kearny?* For the very first time Ballard realized that he had been given a deadline so he would think only about investigating instead of about *why* he was investigating.

"Not that I think it's going to be necessary," Kearny

went on thoughtfully. "Odum will *have* to make his move tonight. And then we'll have him."

"If he doesn't have us first."

"I met a man today who would use Odum for a tooth-pick."

But it wasn't really needed. Ballard had just been talking; he wasn't really nervous any more, or scared, or whatever the hell it had been.

Bart Heslip came out of it, suddenly, all at once, at 9:40 P.M. One minute he was lying there corpselike on the bed, as he had been lying for three days; in the next, his eyes were open, with intelligence struggling for comprehension behind them.

"Hi, Corry," he said vaguely to Corrine Jones. "Jesus, I'm thirsty." And then, to Whitaker's delight, he added so terribly tritely—all the cornball TV doctors had it right —"Where am I? What happened?"

"It's Friday," said Corrine. "Friday night. Oh, Bart—"

"And your name, sir?" asked Whitaker.

"Barton Heslip," he said. "I'm thirsty." His voice sharpened. "What cathouse they let you out of, man?"

Whitaker, in his colorful ensemble that Kearny had noted that morning, looked pained. His hands fluttered. "I am Dr. Arnold Whitaker. This is Trinity Hospital in San Francisco. There is no need to be alarmed. There has been an accident—"

"I'm not alarmed," snapped Heslip in an alarmed voice. "What kind of accident?" Then in awed tones he added, belatedly, "Did you say Friday?"

"Oh, Bart!" Corrine exclaimed again instead of answering. She was clasping one of his hands between her full breasts. More love than she had thought possible possessed her when she looked into his eyes. "Oh, Bart . . ."

The hand tightened within hers. "I've been here since . . . Tuesday?" he asked cautiously.

Giselle, in the background, looked at Whitaker, who nodded. She stepped forward with a wide grin on her face. She'd caught a taxi from the DKA offices as soon as Corinne had called her. "Hi, hotshot," she said.

"Giselle!" Heslip said weakly. "What the hell happened to me?"

"We hoped you could tell us."

He looked at her blankly. "I remember repo'ing the Willets Merc out there on Seventh Avenue . . . telling Larry about it . . ." He looked almost pleadingly at the red-headed nurse. "I'm thirsty . . ."

They parked in a closed gas station a block away from 1902 Gavallo Road in Antioch. It was a small, unenthusiastic delta town, shut up tight here in the residential area although it was not even ten o'clock. Ballard had driven the Ford once past the apartment house, the top story of which was visible over the roofs of the intervening houses.

"We'll walk in," said Kearny. "If the T-Bird's there, we grab it. If not, we check all of the apartments, starting with single women or two girls living together, until somebody pops. Any questions?"

"I need my repo tools?"

"Bring them, but I've got an ignition key dupe. Made it up this morning from the dealer's code numbers."

Although most cars could be hot-wired, keys helped where quick action was necessary. And keys got you around the sticky problem of locking steering wheels activated only by the ignition.

Between the gas station and 1902 Gavallo Road, they met only one other person, a handsome brunette in tight slacks walking a Great Dane that came level with her armpits. Ballard realized he had started to tense up again when Kearny turned to look appreciatively at the girl's taut rump under the clinging trousers: Ballard hadn't even thought of it.

"What happens if he hears us starting the car and starts shooting?"

"Giselle will pay for the flowers out of petty cash."

The bastard, loving it, loving every second of it. No wonder he was so testy around the office. He belonged out here, on the street.

The three-story apartment building was set at right

angles to Gavallo Road, a box with six apartments on each of the upper floors, with laundry rooms, storage lockers, and a dozen numbered parking stalls on the first. These could be reached only from a blacktop driveway which entered the property through the redwood fence and ran the length of the building and around it to the rear. To get to the street from the parking stalls, you had to drive all the way back out around the building.

Which meant there was a chance of being trapped back there if things got hairy.

"Right around in back," said Kearny as they turned in at the gate through the fence, their shoes scuffing the blacktop.

Looking as if you belonged there was the single most important factor in chattel recoveries. Ballard had seen cars repossessed with the registered owner standing in the crowd of gawkers without objecting, merely because of the confidence of the repo man. Kearny went the length of the building as if he were the owner on a tour of inspection. When they had turned down the end of the box, and turned again so they could look down the line of twelve parking stalls, he stopped.

"A car in every one of them."

"And none of them the T-Bird," said Ballard.

A tremendous frustrated anger flushed through him. God*dammit,* wouldn't it *ever* end? Wouldn't they *ever* catch up with Odum, ever find out where Griffin was, even pin down Bart's attacker?

"There's a gap between the front of the building and the fence," said Kearny.

They walked past the stalls. Above their heads, Channel 2's 10:00 P.M. newscast began blaring from an open window. Which car—if any—belonged to Odum's girl friend? Or had Sharon Beaghler conned the great Dan Kearny, too, just as she had conned Larry Ballard earlier?

She hadn't. When they came to the end of the stalls and could look beyond, down the gap between the building and the fence where the garbage pails were, it was there. Gorgeous, the son of a bitch. White over red, hardtop two-door, license 666 KAH.

Ballard's nervousness was gone; he was cold, quick, precise, this was what it was all about. Neither man even slowed down. Kearny had given Ballard the keys; he went for the driver's side. Kearny went down the other side, felt the hood. Knowing whether the motor was cold or warm was often the difference between a flooded engine and a clean grab.

"Hot," said Kearny.

He kept going right around the car as Ballard pulled the door almost shut and twisted the ignition key after turning off the radio. Ballard backed smoothly out, at the same time reaching across to unlock the rider's door. Kearny got in as he put it into drive and pulled away.

"She sounds good," Ballard said to Kearny. He was grinning.

They went down the length of the building, around in front. A man and a woman, silhouetted by the vestibule light, were just coming from the front door as they went by. The man yelled, pointed, then was gone behind them.

"Just in time," said Kearny.

He added nothing to Ballard about a good job, nor did Ballard expect him to. The good job had been in getting there in the first place. Once you spotted the car, it should be yours, short of physical attack by the subject or his friends. Even then, it usually should be yours. You weren't hired to lose them.

"You phone it in to the cops while I make the condition report," said Kearny as they pulled up in the darkened gas station next to the Ford.

Ballard found a dime in his pocket. "Antioch city police or Contra Costa county sheriff's department?"

"Try the sheriff. He'll know who has jurisdiction from the address."

As Ballard stepped into the booth, they heard the sound of a car coming up Gavallo Road, fast. Its lights were on high and the tires shrieked as the people inside it saw the T-Bird in the gas station and stood it on its nose. It was a new yellow Toronado.

"The Lone Ranger and Tonto," said Kearny in a totally unexcited voice.

The driver was a woman, with the streetlight back-lighting her blond hair and casting her features into darkness. The door on the rider's side flew open as the car skidded to a stop. A dark figure hit the concrete running, charging them. Ballard's heart seemed to stop.

"He's got a gun," he heard himself say in a tight, desperately calm voice. "Dan, he's got a gun . . ."

Twenty

It was a monkey wrench.

For the first time Ballard knew why Kearny had such strictures against carrying guns on the job. If he'd had one, he would have used it before realizing that Odum was technically unarmed.

Odum skidded to a stop ten feet away, as if disconcerted that neither of them had run. He was short, burly, very pale, with shaggy hair and glasses thick enough to bottle Cokes in. Tall? thought Ballard. Handsome? Suave? *This* cat?

"Who . . ." Odum stopped and cleared his throat. His voice had come out funny. He was scared shitless. "Who in hell are you?"

Kearny took the play away from him. "Are you Charles M. Griffin?"

"Well, no, I . . ."

"Then it doesn't matter who the hell we are."

Ballard loved to watch him work, take the offensive, push the antagonist in the direction he wanted him to go. Right now he was turning back to the car, leaving Odum with only a broad back in a business suit to argue with.

"I . . . what . . . why the hell did you take this car?" Odum demanded. His girl friend was still in the Toronado, still just a dark shape with the halo of back-lit blond hair.

Kearny turned back to the ex-con. He repeated, in the same harsh tones as before, "Are you Charles M. Griffin?"

"I already told you I wasn't. But—"

"Then it doesn't matter why the hell we took this car."

He turned away again. Odum was emboldened enough to step toward him. Ballard came around the front of the car, fast, fists clenched, but Odum, despite the wrench, wasn't after trouble.

"Well, look, you guys, I . . . ah . . . paid three hundred bucks for the equity in this car. Cash. You can't just—"

"We already have." Kearny turned back, leaned casually against the door with his arms folded, like a farmer talking about crops. "You may as well clear your personal crap out and give us the keys."

"But it's *my* car," said Odum desperately.

"It *can't* be your car." Kearny's voice was patient, reasonable; daddy telling junior about the birds and the bees in words he could understand. "This car belongs to California Citizens Bank and is registered to a Mr. Charles M. Griffin. You aren't either one of 'em."

"But I gave the guy three hundred bucks—"

Kearny leaned forward, arms still folded, but by the sudden tension in his voice and body compelling response. "Griffin?"

Odum was blinking rapidly, as if he were going to cry. "Yeah. That guy. Gloria can vouch—"

"What Gloria says has no validity in a court of law," Kearny said coldly. "Gloria who?"

"Court of law?" Odum's voice was stricken. "Uh . . . Gloria Rouse. She, uh . . . listen, court of . . ."

"The woman in the Toronado?"

"Uh . . . yeah."

"Mm-hmmm." Kearny said it as if a dark suspicion had just been confirmed. "She resides at 1-9-0-2 Gavallo Road, Apartment Seven?"

From the stall in which the yellow Toronado had been parked, of course. That cool bastard must have noted the make of car in *each* stall just walking by, automatically, probably not even aware that his brain was doing it. Ballard couldn't have given him the make of *any* of those cars. Not one.

"Yah . . . uh, yes. Sir."

Sir, added belatedly. Odum, sitting in the straight-backed chair by Saul Savidge's ancient wooden desk, getting told the facts of a parolee's life. Did those showers *really* leak down on the more comfortable swivel chair, or was that just a subtle ploy of Savidge's? *Yes, sir.* Then Ballard thought angrily to himself: Pity for *this* shithead? Who maybe had broken Bart's skull, maybe even with the wrench now dangling forgotten and useless at the end of his arm like the tuft on a jackass's tail?

"You've been living with Gloria Rouse at this address since last Tuesday in clear violation of the conditions of your parole. What sort of explanation can you give for this?"

"I . . ."

His eyes were darting from one to the other, seeking a soft spot. Ballard kept silent, put on his stoniest expression. The normal expression on Kearny's granite features was stony enough.

"I . . . none, sir."

"All right." Kearny made it sound as if he were bestowing a great favor. He turned to Ballard. "Mr. Beam, did Mr. Savidge say anything today about this Thunderbird?"

Ballard hoped he was reading Kearny's lead the right way. "He seemed extremely upset when I told him that the subject might be driving a car, contrary to the conditions of his parole."

"There you are," said Kearny with great finality.

Odum shuffled his feet. "Ah, look, I mean, I hadn't gotten around to telling him yet, but, I . . . look, this week I'll . . ."

"The car isn't yours anyway."

"But I paid three hundred—"

"Where'd you get that from? Kite some more paper?"

"Jesus!" he yelped. "No!"

He said it loud enough to bring the woman out of the car; she wouldn't have been able to hear anything that had gone before. Now she just stood beside it, silent, undecided.

"Does *she* know about you and Sharon Beaghler?" asked Kearny relentlessly, just too low for her to hear.

Odum automatically glanced back at the Toronado.

Seeing her standing beside it, he made almost hysterical waving-away motions with both open hands. She hesitated, finally got back into the car. Which was, Ballard knew, what Kearny had wanted. A cardinal rule of investigating was never to make a man seem unnecessarily foolish or weak in front of his woman. Pride might stiffen otherwise dormant resistance.

Now Kearny laid a comforting hand on the small man's shoulder. "Mr. Odum, we think you've been victimized by an unscrupulous con artist."

"But he gave me a bill of sale and the white—"

"You have those with you?"

"Right here in my wallet . . ." He laid down the monkey wrench on the pavement, got out and riffled through his wallet until he came up with a much-folded rectangle of brown paper that looked like wrapping paper. He also had the white slip for the car—the registration slip which in California designates the registered as opposed to the legal owner of a vehicle.

"See . . ." Odum's blunt cracked fingernail traced the hand-lettered bill of sale and the slanting backhand scrawl, *Charles M. Griffin.*

Kearny looked at him sharply, for a moment not playacting for effect. "Didn't it strike you as odd that he'd give you this sort of butcher-paper receipt and a five-thou car and the white slip for only three hundred bucks? Didn't you suspect that maybe it was hot?"

"He . . . ah . . ." The eyes moved uneasily behind their thick glasses. "He said a new payment book would be mailed to me from the bank. You know, after the transfer of title was recorded, like. I was just s'posed to keep up the payments, and . . . well, see, I was s'posed to send in another two hundred bucks or so, besides the three I give him. That was to pick up those February and March payments, like . . ."

"But you didn't."

"I . . . ran short . . ."

"What did you figure he was going to do when the bank kept on chasing him for the payments?"

The eyes moved again, nervously, from Ballard to

Kearny to the car and back again. He cleared his throat. "Well, ah, see, I was getting his mail, right? And he said he was leaving the country for a year or so, soon as he got the car sold off. So I figured I just wouldn't send those notices on to him when he, ah, you know, sent me his forwarding address . . ."

"He hasn't?" asked Ballard.

"Naw, he never did. Didn't any mail come, either."

"How did he get in touch with you about taking over the equity in the car?"

"He, ah, through a newspaper ad. Just a phone number, it gave, in the Concord paper. I hadda go down to San Jose to see the car. Some tract house, I can't remember the address—"

"1545 Midfield Road?" asked Ballard.

"That's it. After we closed the deal, he, ah, asked me to pick up his mail for him. He said he didn't trust the post office. I didn't want it to come to my rooming house, you know, Savidge has that address, so I thought about Sharon right away. I hadn't met Gloria then yet. Then I forgot to tell Sharon for a couple of weeks . . ."

Which explained the returned letter which had given Kearny the Beaghler address, the returned W-2 which had led Ballard to it.

"Can't I . . . ah . . . keep the car until—"

"No," said Kearny flatly. "Of course, we'll give you *our personal receipt* for both the car and the registration slip. I'm sure you can work something out later with the bank. And meanwhile, Mr. Odum, we'll clear you on the car with Savidge."

"That's right," said Ballard, on cue. "I'll tell him that my informant was mistaken, that it wasn't you driving it after all."

Odum finally shrugged, even grinned wryly. Ballard could see, suddenly, how he had been able to hang paper around a series of East Bay bars. He had a gold tooth right in front; that tooth, with the wide grin and the glasses and the shaggy hair, gave his face a sort of witless charm that suggested he was too dumb to steal.

"Uh . . . Mr. Savidge won't have to know about . . ."

He stopped and jerked a thumb at the Toronado and the blonde waiting inside it.

"Our little secret, Mr. Odum," said Kearny soothingly.

He surrendered the keys; they helped him carry his tool kit over to the Toronado. The tools were the only possessions he had in the car. Gloria Rouse started hassling him angrily as soon as Kearny and Ballard had retreated out of earshot. Ballard called the cops to report the repo; just before he left the booth, the argument ended and the Toronado laid twin streaks of rubber taking off.

"Seven'll get you ten it was her three hundred bucks," said Kearny. "In fact, he probably got the whole five bills from her and then just *told* her he'd sent the other two hundred to the bank."

Ballard agreed. To take even as small a game as Odum, Gloria Rouse would just naturally have to sweeten the pot with money. She was absolutely the ugliest woman he had ever seen, at least from the neck up. He actually found it hard to believe that somebody, sometime, hadn't stuck her in the dog pound by mistake. Maybe somebody had. Maybe that's where Odum had gotten her. Went in for a collie, came out with Gloria Rouse.

Kearny was still staring pensively after the departed car. "Well, what do you think? Still like little Howie as that topless dancer's weirdo with the flashlight? What did she call him? Tall? Dark? Handsome? This guy looks like he's been in a closet for twenty years."

"Odum must have *something,* Dan. Sharon Beaghler—"

Kearny shook his head impatiently. "She'll drop her pants for anything that can get stiff. Just the fact that her old man doesn't like Odum would be enough to turn her on to him."

"So we're right back where we started? It was Griffin all along? And we don't have lead one as to where Griffin is—except that he was supposed to have left the country. Who don't we have extradition treaties with any more?"

"Not quite back where we started." Kearny got into the T-Bird. "We've got this. And we're pretty sure Odum is out of it. And we know that if Griffin left the country, he came back—at least *somebody* knocked Bart on the head. I'll drive down to Concord to my wagon, throw this on the tow bar, and bring it in tomorrow morning. You'd better go home and get some sleep."

"Big deal," grunted Ballard, with a terrible sense of anticlimax.

Twenty-one

How could they have missed so badly? As he began the fifty-mile drive to San Francisco, Ballard mentally reworked the other five cases he had closed in his search for Bart's attacker. Had he screwed up on one of those? Or had the attacker actually come from some other case entirely? Or from some incident in Bart's life that nobody —maybe not even Bart—would know about?

Or were the police right after all? Had Bart taken out the Jag for some unknown personal reason and gone off Twin Peaks by accident?

No, dammit, he couldn't accept that. There had to be something he had missed or misinterpreted in the Griffin file, something even Kearny had missed or misinterpreted, something that would lead them to . . .

He realized that he had listened twice to his own name being called on the radio by an unfamiliar voice.

"Uh, yeah, this is SF-6. Over." Panic nibbled at him. Bart . . .

"Are you Larry Ballard?"

"10-4. Larry Ballard. Go ahead, please."

"This is Dunlop Jensen, NFS. Giselle Marc of KDM 366 asked me to relay a message to you from San Francisco, over."

NFS. News Forwarding Service. Ballard remembered Giselle talking about this guy. A house-bound cripple who lived up in the hills behind Oakland and made a living monitoring scores of local radio bands, picking up reports of fire, robberies, emergencies, relaying them to Bay

Area TV stations for a per-item fee and to emergency services *gratis*.

"Did you read my last transmission, SF-6? Over."

"Loud and clear, NFS. Go ahead with the message from KDM 366."

Ballard was amazed his voice was so even. Dread was clutching at him. Giselle wouldn't be on the DKA radio at midnight unless something had happened. Bart . . . dead? Or maybe worse, Bart waking up with mashed potatoes where his brains had been? Since Oakland Control would be shut down and SF Control hadn't been able to reach them here, far beyond the East Bay hills, Giselle had used Dunlop Jensen as a relay.

"Here is the message," came Jensen's voice. " 'Bart is sitting in with a full deck.' KDM 366 said you would know what this meant."

What it meant? Jesus, Jesus, it meant Bart was awake and all right! It meant . . .

"10-4! Message received and understood. Do you drink bourbon, over?"

"Anything I can get, SF-6." There was immediate warmth in the voice at Ballard's personal question. "I've got the original hollow leg. Two of 'em, in fact. Literally."

"Giselle and a bottle and I will be up on Sunday."

"I'll be here," said Jensen happily, and signed off.

Ballard's foot went down, sending the Ford toward the Bay Bridge at a speed that would have gotten him a ticket if the CHP unit patrolling that stretch of freeway hadn't been stopped for coffee in the all-night café at Orinda Village.

The T-Bird had no citizens' band, so Kearny did not hear the exchanges between Ballard and Dunlop Jensen. He was loafing along at a sedentary sixty, listening to KEEN Radio's country and western out of San Jose, tapping time against the steering wheel with his fingers. If some of Ballard's frustration at the dead end in the Charles M. Griffin investigation also burned in his gut, he gave no outward sign of it. He had been around a long time, knew himself well enough to control impatience.

Not that knowing yourself helped a hell of a lot in the detective business. Knowing *other* people was the secret, knowing enough to ease off on Parker, to ease off on Hawkley, to keep pushing on Griffin. He'd never ease off on *that* son of a bitch because, unlike Ballard, he had no momentary fears that they might have gotten the wrong case.

They had the right case. They just hadn't gotten it turned right side up yet. Heslip had been attacked: the attack had been perpetrated, as the police would say, either *by* Griffin or *because* of Griffin.

So go back to Griffin, then. Start with the given information.

A big, usually easygoing guy with a mother fixation, early forties, balding, muttonchop sideburns, drinking too much, six feet tall and 210 pounds, physically well able to clout Heslip over the head, carry him to the Jaguar, run him off Twin Peaks.

Physically able. But was he the head-roller *type*? A man like Parker, okay. But Griffin? Hard to accept. Could a guy called sweet by a big lusty broad he had walked out on, a guy hung up on Mom and apple pie and the missionary position, become so devious, so larcenous, so money-hungry as to embezzle, over a period of years, thirty thousand bucks?

Something flickered through a corner of his mind, too fast to catch, even though his foot came off the accelerator momentarily and he eased into the right lane. He shook his head and picked up speed again. Missed it.

Back to the contradictory Griffin. And his mother. She died, freeing him at last for the swinging bachelor life. Booze, the big lush topless dancer, a big sedately sporty car. Joy at being free? Or desperation at being alone? Clinging to Cheri as a cockeyed mother substitute? Something there? What about him telling Cheri he was going to "do something" about the kink with the flashlight?

Kearny shook his head again. Chivalry didn't fit with Griffin's animal cunning in confusing his back trail. It didn't fit with his murderous ability to make murderous decisions and carry them out under the goad of panic.

It was as if he were two different guys. As if . . .

Kearny swerved the T-Bird abruptly into the right lane, slowing as he checked the rear-view mirror, letting it roll dead on the shoulder. Griffin, acting like a split personality—what did the head-shrinkers call it, a schizoid personality? One shocked by his kinky friend's attempted assault on Cheri, the other turning around and selling the furniture she was using. There was the answer, of course. And there was an easy way to find out if he was right or not. Ask Odum the questions he should have asked the first time, as soon as he had realized that Odum was guilty of nothing more than his own native stupidity.

Kearny pulled back into the deserted freeway, went on swiftly to the first overpass which would let him wishbone back toward Antioch. Toward Howard Odum and his ugly girl friend. Toward the answers to two questions.

Not that they would clear up all the problems. But they would confirm *who*—if he was right; and if he was, they would confirm *why* Bart had gotten it. Because Bart had been close, very close, without even realizing there was anything to be close to. Had stopped, of course, just to be a nice guy. *I got something funny on one of the files, probably just a coincidence . . .*

Which it hadn't been. It had been deadly.

Yes, Kearny was getting old, soft between the ears. To miss such obvious answers concerning the whole San Jose episode. Misdirection. Making the dead appear alive days, even weeks, after the actual death. Which had been, Kearny figured, on February 9.

It was after midnight when he went up the walk to 1902 Gavallo Road in Antioch. He was turning over in his mind the four possible methods for getting through the locked front door of the building in a hurry, but none of them was necessary. Just as he got there a grumpy-faced man in a bathrobe and slippers was dragged out by a long-haired Chihuahua the size and general configuration of a squirrel.

The dog yapped in ferocious challenge as Kearny caught the door before its pneumatic closer did. The detective beamed and said "Good evening" at the same time the sour-faced man said, "Every goddamn night at midnight. Every goddamn night."

Kearny nodded and kept smiling and kept going, up the inner stairs to the top floor, turning left to number seven. He took a wrench out of his pocket—brought along for method three of getting into the building, breaking out a pane of glass—and began tapping with it on the hollow-core birch door. He kept on tapping, neither louder nor softer, faster nor slower, until a strangled angry voice called from within.

A few moments later the door was wrenched open and Odum, minus his glasses and unexpectedly hairy in hastily donned shorts, peered out. "I oughta bust in your nose, buddy, this time of night! I—"

"Two questions I should have asked before." Kearny's heavy uncompromising voice was full of an inevitability few could withstand. Odum, he knew, could not. Odum was a born loser; he'd be back inside before the year was out. He would always go for the wrong decision as a moth would always go for a candle.

The myopic eyes had finally recognized Kearny. "Oh!" he exclaimed, "I didn't . . . I thought . . . Ah . . . what are the questions?"

"One. What did Griffin look like? Two. Did you give his description to a black investigator named Heslip on Tuesday afternoon?"

And Odum answered them.

Ten minutes later Kearny was in the Thunderbird and picking up an on-ramp for California 4 west. No time now to bury Griffin's car in Concord while he picked up his station wagon. If someone tried to get him on the radio they couldn't, of course—but who would be on the air this time of night anyway?

No, he'd just drive the T-Bird into the city, stop somewhere to check a phone book, get the address. If it was an unlisted number, stop at the DKA office to check the city directory. Because Odum's answers had confirmed it.

The killer hadn't just been stupid; he just hadn't realized how complex people's lives were. Hadn't known that being docketed for a court appearance, and being out on $600 bail, coupled with the disappearance, would send a lawyer and an insurance agent and finally a firm of private detectives snooping into Griffin's life. And talk about stupid: why hadn't Kearny realized long before that Griffin had used the Castro Valley address in good faith on his credit application for the T-Bird, even though he had moved out the month before? It probably still was his *legal* residence, because he would have owned it once the will cleared probate. He probably still had been registered to vote out of that address. A shame. A damned shame.

At least Bart hadn't died. Yet. Kearny would call the hospital later, maybe even drop in there after he had wrapped up the case. No need to ask Bart what he had done after leaving Odum on Tuesday afternoon. Kearny already knew. He hoped the body wouldn't be too hard to find. He had a pretty good idea of where it would be. The simplistic reason for selling the furniture told him that. And, of course, the fact that the killer seemed always to act under the grip of emotion. Strike first, consider the consequences later, as he had done with Bart.

Twenty-two

The fog was in, ponderous and wet, when Ballard parked
on Bush, went in the ambulance entrance of Trinity
Hospital. Fifty paces through the misty fog had furred his
clothes and hair with moisture. He wiped his face with
his handkerchief as he pushed the button; the elevator
was slow enough so he had gotten two Mr. Goodbars
from the candy machine, had bolted one and was crunch-
ing on the other before it arrived.

The third-floor hall was warm, quiet, dim except for
the hard white light from the duty desk at the far end.
A bulky white shape came from behind the desk; he
recognized the gimlet-eyed nurse who'd been shocked at
Whitaker's language on Wednesday morning. Wednesday? Seemed weeks rather than days ago. Involuntarily,
he gave a huge yawn.

"Mr. Ballard?" she asked in a hushed angry whisper.

"That's right."

"Well . . . Doctor said you could go in," she said
grudgingly. "Visiting time was over *hours* ago . . ."

For a moment Ballard thought the radio message had
been a cruel hoax. Heslip still lay as silent as before. His
eyes were still shut, his head was still swathed in bandages.
Then Ballard saw the look on Corinne's face as she started
to her feet, and he knew it was all right.

"He just fell asleep waiting for you to get here," said
Whitaker.

The jaunty little doctor was sitting on the arm of
Giselle Marc's chair, one arm across the back of it and

thus draped loosely around her shoulders, the fingers of the other hand resting with artful casualness on one of her bare forearms. The tall blonde looked bemused, like a greyhound under amorous assault by a Pekingese.

"You got my radio message?" She seemed delighted with the diversion Ballard provided.

"From Dunlop Jensen? Yeah. I promised him a bottle of booze."

She stood up with a lithe, quick movement, smoothed down her short plaid wool skirt. "Want me to go with you when you deliver it?"

"I've already volunteered you."

He turned toward Corinne, almost warily. She reached up to put her fingertips against the side of his neck.

"You know I'm sorry, don't you, Larry? Giselle told me—"

Ballard put his arms around her. She clung fiercely to him. Whitaker cleared his throat as a somewhat wan voice came from the bed.

"Hands off the woman, honky."

Without releasing Corinne, Ballard turned to look down at Heslip. He let his eyes move over the still form under the blankets, from bandaged crown to toe and back again. Then he slowly shook his head in disbelief. "It looks like it was strained through a handkerchief."

"I hear you've been working my assignments, screwing them up."

"Trying to get them *unscrewed* from the mess you left them in."

Ballard let go of Corinne and went around the bed to the head of it. He made a fist and touched Heslip's cheekbone with it, then reached behind him to pull up a spare chair and sit down.

"Dan wanted to bring you a watermelon as soon as you woke up," he said, "but I took him over to East Bay and lost him. Last I saw he was driving a red and white T-Bird—"

"You mean the *Griffin* car?" exclaimed Heslip.

"*Griffin!*" yelped Giselle. "You got Griffin?"

"We got his car," said Ballard. He turned back to

Heslip. "How much do you remember about Tuesday night?" He looked over to Whitaker. "Or aren't I supposed to ask?"

"Ask," said Whitaker. He waved the chromed watch. Ballard wondered if the wife had gotten him into the bathtub yet. "There's mental shock connected with this sort of injury and coma, a disorientation that can be quite devastating to the patient. The more that he can place himself in time and event without becoming agitated, the better for his own peace of mind."

"Oh *no!*" wailed Corinne softly. "Not you too, Doctor! Not *tonight!*"

Whitaker gave an apologetic shrug.

Heslip was frowning. "I've been trying to . . . get it together since they told me what happened. Truth is, I coulda actually *been* driving that damn Jaguar for all I can remember . . ."

"Remember talking to me on the radio?"

"I remember the Willets repo, I remember . . . yeah, I remember telling you about it. I was gonna meet you at the office, right?"

"Right."

"Giselle, can't you stop them?" asked Corinne, as if she hated the idea of Heslip even talking about it.

Giselle looked over at Whitaker. He gave no reaction, so she shrugged wryly. "I'm as bad as they are, Corinne. I want to hear."

"Do you remember working the Griffin case on Tuesday?" asked Ballard.

That Heslip remembered. He had seen Leo at JRS Garage in the morning, had gotten the California Street address in Concord; that had seemed not enough to warrant a run over there. He usually would have just turned it over to the Oakland office, but on a dead skip like Griffin any field agent would love to turn him alone, thus giving a not too subtle finger to the field agents working out of the office of origin.

"Did you talk to a girl named Cheri?" asked Ballard.

He hadn't. He'd dug out the landlady, found out about the accident to the T-Bird, had gone to the Concord cops and asked them what garage it had been towed to after the Christmas Eve smash. Ballard just shook his head on that one. Jesus! Some investigator he was! Heslip had made all the moves that Ballard *should* have made.

"Doctor, can't *you* stop them?" demanded Corinne.

Whitaker looked at his watch and nodded thoughtfully. "It *is* late, and he *does* need rest."

"Cat at the garage had a mailing address on Griffin," said Heslip.

The address Ballard had been able to get only round-about, through Harvey E. Wyman, insurance agent. At the Beaghler house, Heslip had seen the kids playing in the yard and had talked with them. They knew all about the T-Bird, knew "Howie" drove it and had been in prison. When Sharon had come back from the laundro-mat, Heslip had said he was an ex-con just out of stir, and she had given him the address of the rooming house in Concord. Just like that. Any friend of Howie's . . .

"And you talked with Odum," said Ballard in total self-disgust. He didn't even make it a question.

"I think that's enough now," said Whitaker.

Both men jumped; they had been in that shared pro-fessional world from which Corinne was excluded be-cause she was without the manhunting instincts they had, that Giselle had, that Kearny epitomized.

"I talked with him," said Heslip quickly. "Didn't get anything out of him; he said he dropped the car off at the garage in April for a guy he met in a bar. Griffin, of course. Only the description he gave me was a phony . . ." He stopped there, an odd remembering look on his face.

Ballard stood up guiltily; he didn't want to cause a repalse or some damned thing.

Heslip was frowning again. "I keep thinking that on the way back . . . I stopped . . . *somewhere* . . ."

"Out," said Whitaker in a suddenly no-nonsense doc-torish voice. Corinne had gotten a smile of triumph on her face, when he turned to her also. "Even you, my sweet, my love. The crisis is past. Shoo."

"But . . . he *needs* me, he . . ."

"Out out out—before the nurse reports me to the AMA."

". . . remember talking with the cop on that Willets repo," said Heslip dreamily. "I . . . yeah! Left my damned case sheets out above the visor of the Plymouth . . ."

"And you went out to get them?" supplied Ballard. "And . . . what?"

"And nothing," said Heslip ruefully. His eyelids were drooping again. "I went out to get them . . . I turned around . . . And baby, it was Friday night . . ."

Ballard let himself be herded easily; it was Giselle who held back. She started explaining that they *had* to probe Bart's memory for anything else he could remember of that Tuesday night, but Whitaker just shook his head. "He never will, my dear. Not ever. I'm amazed he can recall as close to the moment of impact as he can. Most unusual. A remarkably well-balanced mind to penetrate its own defenses as far as it has."

He paused; and then a look of beatific evil suffused his features. He thrust out a pointing arm in the classic, old-time gesture. He ended with a quivering forefinger pointing down the hall toward the blinding snowstorm obligatory to all such scenes. "Do not darken my doorway again," he said to Giselle in a thunderously Victorian voice. "I am *not* the father of your child!"

"*Doc*tor!" gasped Gimlet-Eyes, just passing on her rounds.

But Whitaker had firmly shut the door in all of their faces.

"He doesn't under*stand!*" exclaimed Corinne disconsolately. "Bart *needs* me, he's going to have a bad night, he—"

"He needs *sleep*," said Gimlet-Eyes triumphantly. "And from now on, *you* will have to observe normal visiting hours like everyone else."

The nurse stopped; she had lost Ballard. He was over at the duty desk, delving behind the counter with a long arm.

"Oh!" She charged him, her several corpulences jouncing to make Corinne break into sudden giggles. "What are you doing? You get away from that counter . . ."

"Phone book," said Ballard curtly. When she didn't respond, he snapped his fingers under her nose impatiently. "Come on, come on. Phone book."

She got him a phone book, almost meekly. No telling *what* sort of disturbance he would cause if she *didn't*. And no use appealing to Dr. Whitaker, either; he was as eccentric as the rest of them.

If the murderer wasn't in the phone book, had an unlisted number, say, he'd have to go all the way back downtown to the DKA office, get the city directory and hope that . . .

No. Here he was, 27 Java Street.

Java Street? Hell. Ballard didn't know where Java Street was. And if it wasn't within walking distance of Twin Peaks, say twenty minutes walk at the outside . . .

He needed a city map. Had one down in the car . . .

"Sir, you're going to *have* to leave—"

"Huh? What? Oh. Yeah." He flipped the phone book shut on top of the counter, turned away, organizing his face into a belatedly casual expression for Giselle's sharp eyes. "Sure. Thanks."

". . . don't really want you to bother with running me home," Giselle was saying to Corinne.

"It would be really *no* bother, Giselle." Corinne looked suddenly exhausted, blasted, as if by release from the tension which had sustained her.

"I'll have Larry drive me across the Bay." Giselle had never learned how to drive; none of the field agents had the patience to teach her. Her very blue eyes were narrowed slightly, fixed on Ballard with intense speculation. "He won't mind, will you, Larry?"

"Mind what?" he said, trying to duck out of it. Dammit, it would kill an hour altogether, going and coming.

"Driving me over to Oakland tonight."

"I'm, ah . . . pretty exhausted myself, Giselle." He started a fake yawn, ended up with a real jaw-creaker that wasn't faked at all. He *was* damned tired, but he had to get into that house, the proof that Griffin was dead might be there somewhere. "If you're short cab fare . . ."

"I will not ride a cab, Larry Ballard, when you're here with a perfectly good DKA car burning DKA gas . . ."

"As long as Corinne offered—"

"I'm riding with you," she said with finality. "Corinne is going home and going to sleep. She hasn't slept for days."

Corinne was looking from one to the other with an unbelieving look on her face.

"I don't understand you people," she said weakly. "I really don't understand anything about you."

"Lots of times I don't understand us myself," said Giselle.

Corinne smiled her brilliant smile. "But I'm sure glad he's going to drive you home. All of a sudden, I'm just dead."

What the hell, he'd just have to swallow that extra hour's delay. He'd dump Giselle, come back. Java Street *had* to be close enough to Twin Peaks for it to have worked; nothing else, no*body* else fit. Heslip, after all, had turned around.

He grabbed Giselle's arm. "Well, c'mon, you're in such a rush to get home."

Giselle went with him meekly. Too meekly. He should have known.

Twenty-three

They rode down in the elevator silently, each busy with his own thoughts. The outside air was wet, the wind penetrating, so Giselle shivered despite the London Fog waterproof she had on over her wool skirt and short-sleeved sweater. She and Ballard walked Corinne to her car; the stop lights on the corner of Scott half a block away were red and green blobs through the fog.

" 'When shall we three meet again?' " Giselle asked rhetorically.

Corinne stuck her head out of the place where the Triumph's window had been until six months before, when some mother-of-a-car-booster had smashed it out for a big score: a pack of Winstons in the glove box. " 'In thunder, lightning, or in rain,' " she quoted back with a flash of perfect teeth in her dark face.

Ballard watched the taillights recede into the soup, then walked back to his Ford, held the door for Giselle, and started the heater as soon as the motor was running. "Soon as we warm this up we'll get you over to Oakland."

"Thanks a lot," she said.

The sarcasm of her tone was lost on Ballard. He was thinking of the San Francisco map over Giselle's visor. Could he get it down, casually, look up Java Street? No, dammit, he'd have to wait until he dumped her off. If she knew where he planned to go, she'd go all DKA official on him or—worse yet—want to go along.

Giselle shivered. She was feeling very Bardish that night. " 'Tis now the very witching time of night, and hell itself breathes out contagion to this world.' " She paused, breathed out. "See? It's cold enough to see your breath."

"You talk too much," said Ballard.

"That's because I'm scared. I don't get out into the field all that often, and when I do, it usually isn't after a would-be murderer."

"What the hell is that supposed to mean?" he snapped.

But she already had reached up for the map he had been eyeing wistfully a few moments before. She opened it and looked over at him sweetly. "Which street is it?"

"I don't know what you're talking about."

Her blue eyes were very direct and challenging even by the fog-dimmed streetlights. "Get off it, hotshot. I've been in this business a lot more years than you even if we *are* the same age. So don't try to con *me*. You let Whitaker herd you out of that room as meek as a lamb —which means you thought something Bart said had given it to you. Outside, you made a beeline for a phone book to look up an address. When we got into the car just now your hands were shaking, you wanted to reach for that map so badly. So . . . what street is it?"

Ballard stared at her, silently raging, then sighed. "Java."

"Java . . ." She consulted the index, folded the map open to the appropriate coordinates by the overhead light he had switched on. "It is one block long, runs between . . . Masonic and Buena Vista Avenue West."

"Dead-ends in Buena Vista Park?" demanded Ballard, finally able to visualize the street. He had been afraid it would be way to hell out in the Mission District with Brazil and Persia and Russia and France.

"That's the one. But what difference does the area make if . . . Of course!" she exclaimed. "It would have to be within walking distance of Twin Peaks, wouldn't it?"

Ballard nodded. "So he could walk home after putting Bart over the edge in the Jaguar. Couldn't *tow* the Jag up there—somebody might remember. Couldn't call a cab, same reason—or even walk down to where he could catch a cruiser . . ."

"Dan had me check out every cab company's trip sheets for Wednesday A.M.," Giselle said thoughtfully.

Trust Kearny. He didn't miss many. "And?"

"None at all from anywhere reasonably near Twin Peaks during the right time span." She paused. "Why are we just sitting here?"

"Oh. Sorry." He started the car. "I'll get you home and—"

She neatly twitched the key from the ignition and sat back with it in her hand as the Ford *ca-chunked* to a stop in the middle of Bush Street.

"Uh-uh, hotshot. I'm going with."

"Like hell you are."

"You aren't enough man to put me out of this car."

He stared out the windshield, rubbed his hand down over his whisker-bristled face. Damn, he was tired. Well? Either she went along or he didn't go tonight. What the hell, she was better than most men he knew at this business. Better than him, come to think of it, in everything except the occasional physical stuff. And who knew what he would find at Java Street? He didn't even know if the guy was married or single. He might have a shack-up there for the night, might be throwing a party, might . . .

He put out his hand, wordlessly. Wordlessly, she laid the key in it. He was suddenly glad to have the bright, rangy blonde beside him in the car. "It *was* something Bart said," he told her. "I still don't know how the killer got on to Bart, but—"

"You keep saying killer. Bart isn't dead." He realized how far behind in the case she was; she knew nothing of his and Kearny's day in the East Bay. Then her eyes widened. "I . . . see. So you think Charles Griffin is . . ."

Ballard jogged the Ford over to the 000 block of Masonic; the big dark silent Sears store hulked dimly through the ranks of fog marching up from the ocean.

"Buried in the basement of 27 Java Street," he said. "Or somewhere on the property. I hope. Because without him we don't have any proof of anything, not even now."

"We can show the murderer to Cheri Tart," Giselle suggested.

"Identify him as Mr. Kink with the flashlight? What good would that do?"

But what about showing him to Howard Odum? He must have posed as Griffin in San Jose while getting rid of the car. The car had been the weak point all along. It had to disappear to make Griffin's disappearance plausible; he hadn't realized he could have just abandoned it on the street.

Java Street.

Narrow, almost an alley between two fog-swept and night-deserted streets. At the far end, as Ballard turned off Masonic, was the dark steep mass of Buena Vista park rising ghostlike into the mist. He turned off the engine; the silence was very loud. A gout of fog swept densely across the windshield, momentarily blotting out everything beyond the nose of the car as if it were a ship which had buried its prow in a monstrous gray sea. He'd killed lights and motor and ghosted up to the far curb thirty feet beyond the address.

"I just hope I can recognize fresh concrete if I see it."

Giselle shivered. "How do you plan to get us in?" With the motor and heater killed, the wet cold was seeping quickly through her.

"Bust something if I have to. I'll take a tire iron. And that's singular, Giselle."

"What am I supposed to do? Sit in the car and listen to the radio?" she demanded bitterly.

"Use your head. I need somebody covering me."

She thought about it. Finally she sighed. He was right. "I'll try to raise Dan on the radio, or any of the other field men. And if I see anyone fitting the murderer's description—"

"A long blast on the horn. Just one. And lock the doors. This guy seems to panic and then make decisions fast—and act on them even faster."

"I'll scream a real scream," said Giselle coolly.

Ballard got out, got a tire iron from the trunk. The fog was so thick that to the watching Giselle, it turned

DEAD SKIP / 163

him into a mere dim moving form by the time he reached the far curb.

Giselle switched her attention to the house. No lights, of course, or they would have abandoned the plan. It was a massive square white wood structure with broad front steps leading up to an arched pillared entryway with a wide heavy wood door. She counted the steps. Eleven of them.

In the process she lost Ballard. Well, he'd probably go around to the back, through the heavy bushes which flanked both sides of the house. A double lot, of course, most of these old houses had that. Three stories, the windows on the second floor very big, those on the third, narrow garret-type openings. And on the right-hand front corner of the house a round three-story turret, made of wood and shingles, with a peaked roof like a dunce cap. Curved tall windows, curtained, looking down from the turret.

She looked quickly ahead, toward the park, over her shoulder. Nothing lived except swirling fog. She switched on the ignition, watched the red right glow from the radio. It was comforting, familiar; she didn't feel as brash as she had when Larry had been there.

"KDM 366 Control calling SF-1. Come in, Dan."

No response, not that she expected any. Kearny would be home in bed in Lafayette, the T-Bird tucked into the Kearny double garage. Kearny had a radio unit in a converted closet off the bedroom where he and Jeanie slept, but a mobile unit wouldn't reach that far. Only SF and Oakland Controls.

Still, she conscientiously tried him twice more. No answer.

"KDM 366 Control calling any SF unit."

Again, nothing. Nobody out at 2:00 A.M. on a Saturday, which wasn't surprising. Not this early in the month. Besides, Larry and Bart were the best DKA nighthawks anyway, the ones who took chances, who thought it was fun as well as a job. Bart was in the hospital and Larry was inside the house at 27 Java Street by now. Had been gone long enough to be inside. Breaking and entering.

Giselle shook her head. Just as good she hadn't gotten Kearny, really. If he knew what Ballard was doing, he'd skin Larry alive. And skin Giselle Marc, too. She knew better, knew the consequences of this sort of unplanned action if anything went wrong.

Emotionally involved on this one, all of them. Running around in circles from the beginning, ignoring the *facts,* ignoring the *evidence.* And because of it, working from a massively wrong premise right from the beginning, from the first note Larry wrote on the case. Even before that, from the verbal she had gotten from Heslip on Tuesday afternoon.

They had assumed that Griffin had disappeared because he had embezzled a large sum of money from JRS Garage. Which was wrong, dead wrong. Larry had realized that as soon as he knew who the murderer was.

No, Griffin had disappeared because he *hadn't* embezzled any money. And because his mother had died and he had started drinking heavily. (She and Ballard were wrong in this reasoning, but they weren't to know that until it was too late.)

Anyway, she thought, because they were involved in the case personally, and were working from a wrong assumption, they had ignored the most obvious evidence that Griffin wasn't an embezzler and never had been. His chronically delinquent auto payments. A man smart enough to embezzle a large sum of money would have used some of it to keep his account current and thus not draw attention to himself needlessly.

She drew her coat tighter around her. Cold in the car, without the motor or the heater on. But she couldn't run them, couldn't even smoke. Not on a deadly serious stakeout like this one.

Movement froze her. Then she gave a nervous little giggle. A gray-and-white-striped tomcat had run across the street from her side and into the bushes on the edge of the property at 27 Java.

She tried Kearny again on the radio, tried the other SF field men. No answer. Nobody abroad this night except a gray-and-white cat, chased or frightened out from under Ballard's car . . .

Chased or frightened by what?

And then she realized, just too late, that she hadn't pushed down the lock button on the driver's side after Larry had gotten out. She lunged across the seat, but as her fingers grazed the door, it was jerked open and a dark bulky shape came into the car at her. She didn't even have time to scream, let alone hit the horn ring.

Twenty-four

Ballard paused in the shadows of the dripping bushes that flanked the walk. No lights showed in the house, but that didn't mean nobody was home. It was two o'clock in the morning. The bars were just closing and . . . He gave a little snort. Just seventy-two hours since Bart had gotten it, and here he was, at the killer's house.

Why, really? Because he wanted to close this one out all by himself? Partially. But also because the murderer might find out that Bart Heslip was still alive. If Griffin *was* buried here, the killer might have left traces he would hide or obliterate, not knowing that Bart was permanently blacked out on what he had seen when he had been struck.

He shot one glance between sodden leaves back at the car. Just a dim shape across the street. From behind, Giselle's head would be hidden by the high-backed seat. It made him feel rather secure to know Giselle was there to warn him with a horn blast if anyone fitting the murderer's description showed up.

Ballard boldly mounted the broad front steps, eleven of them, and gently turned the front doorknob. Locked, of course. It wasn't the foolhardy maneuver it seemed; he knew his rubber-soled shoes made little noise on the steps or the porch itself.

Door locked, no garage to give possible access. Around in back, then.

The lot wasn't a great deal wider than the house, even though it was a double, but the property was deep. He had to use his flashlight three times on the journey along

166

the side of the house to keep from tripping over bushes or roots. The ground rose sharply under his feet; a hillside lot, backed up against the broad base of Twin Peaks.

The back door was locked, although the wood of the frame was so old that it almost gave when he laid his weight against it. Ten seconds with his tire iron would have had it open, but they would have been noisy seconds.

Better to try the windows first. Because of the slope of the lot, the sills of the rear windows were at waist-level rather than far above his head as they had been at the front.

The third one he tried was unlocked.

But it was stuck. He worked on it with the tire iron, digging it into the wood and gently prying upward, and within a few moments it had broken free. He pushed up the bottom half, then melted back into the bushes behind the house.

Ballard had prowled houses before, of course; nobody spent very long in the investigation game without an occasional crude illegal-entry job—through attached garages if nowhere else. Usually it was just curiosity, the almost unnatural interest in delving behind people's façades that most detectives seemed to have.

Curiosity. What killed the cat. And he was dealing with a killer.

No lights went on, no second-story windows went up, no pale questing faces appeared. After two minutes Ballard moved in again. If anyone was there, he was asleep. Or lying in ambush.

Ashcan that, Ballard. Time to do it.

He wiped his hands down his pant legs before swinging a leg up over the sill, then went in under the white lacy curtains that covered the opening. When he straightened up he was in a disused dining room. A single stab of flashlight showed a heavy oak table, big captain's chair at the head and lesser chairs ranged down the sides. An immense oak sideboard with a collection of bottles on it. Behind it, a big mirror with an ornate frame.

Ballard wiped his hands again. He was totally illegal now, totally vulnerable. If the bastard walked in on him now and shot him, the cops couldn't do a damned thing about it except sweep him up and cart him away.

Better not to think about that. If the killer wasn't in here, asleep, Giselle would give warning if he showed up.

He crossed the room by the flashlight, switched it out before opening the door. The air in the hall was fresher; the dining room, then, was usually shut up. Which suggested a man living alone. He wished he'd had time to research this guy a little.

The hell of it was, he was scared. Heart thumping.

Light from the street came through the heavy etched glass half-panel of the front door despite the fog. By it, Ballard could see that the hallway ran straight back through the house to the kitchen in the rear. He stood in front of the dining-room door, mouth-breathing. No sound, not anywhere in the house. No *feel* of anyone in the house.

The kitchen was old-fashioned, with a wooden drainboard flanking the stained porcelain sink. Water heater, new icebox, new electric stove. He opened a couple of drawers at random. Silverware. Knives. A heavy-caliber blue-steeled revolver. A homeowner's weapon. Ballard checked it. No shells. He left it there. A tire iron was a better weapon than an empty gun.

Peanut-butter jar open on the table beside the toaster. Small plate, butter-smeared knife, coffee cup with a half-inch of mud in the bottom, everything seen in circular segments by his moving flashlight.

Breakfast remains; so he hadn't eaten supper here. Hadn't returned from work, maybe. Which suggested the probability that Ballard had the place to himself but might not for much longer.

So get moving.

The door which opened off the hall beside the kitchen door showed utter blackness and stairs going down. Cellar. Where he wanted to go, after making sure he was alone. Burning sensation between the shoulder blades. He worked his shoulders to ease it. Tension.

Past the dining-room door. Next, same side of the hall, the study. Empty. Next, living room. Empty. Old, heavy, cumbersome, perhaps valuable furniture. Antiques, probably. Probably inherited along with the house. A baby grand piano. Well dusted. Probably had a woman in once a week. He sure as hell could afford it.

The stairway to the second floor was just to the left of the front door as you entered from the street. Wide hardwood treads, so solid they didn't creak though they must have been there at least half a century. The banisters were also hardwood, polished by generations of hands.

On the second floor the hall ran across the width of the house rather than down its length. Six doors opened off it, three on each side. So dark that Ballard had to use the flashlight, first to guide himself to each door and then to guide his hand to the knob. He was sweating profusely. If anyone was here, on this floor this was where they would be.

Bathroom. Empty. Modern fixtures, all redone. Men's toilet articles. Across the hall to the street-side room. A bedroom, fixed up into a study. New, modern furniture, bright colors, vinyls and naugahyde, Swedish modern desk and chairs. Money had gone into it. Well, he had money, right?

Middle rear, another bedroom, unused. Must have been his as a kid, pennants on the wall, street signs, faded photos of Forty-Niners who had retired. The Lion, Hurricane Hugh, Y.A. An odd monument to an innocent past.

Middle front room, very careful opening the door, single flash of the light to show it was a bedroom with a big unmade king-size bed. Ballard made a quick check of the two walk-in closets. Lots of clothes, all men's clothes, good ones. Ten pairs of highly polished shoes. He went to the window, checked the street by carefully drawing aside the curtain. He could see the roof of his car. The fog was as thick and wet-looking as before. Everything serene. Everything muffled.

Final rear room was a darkroom, a hell of a good one —all the chemicals, a Zeiss enlarger that looked new, storage racks with photo paper. A photography buff, too.

Which left the sixth door. Ballard tried this cautiously: locked. He looked at the join between frame and door.

Dried. A gap there. He inserted the spatulate end of his tire iron and exerted steady gradually increasing pressure against the lock. It gave. The door was open. Spiral stairs led up, which made it the entrance to the third-floor turret room. What the hell. Better make sure.

He checked his watch. It was 2:17. He had been inside less than fifteen minutes. It seemed like fifteen hours.

These stairs creaked, so he took his time on them, tried to stay on the outside edge, against the wall. The treads were not hardwood, uncarpeted, unswept. Not a place the cleaning lady was allowed to come, which quickened Ballard's pulse and made him move with great caution. Jimmying the door had made some noise, even if not much.

The door at the top of the stairs was closed but unlocked. When he eased it open, enough light came through the filmy curtains on the narrow curved windows to show him the place was empty. He went in, saw it was a photo gallery. He crossed the room to the wall, suddenly stopped dead when he realized what the big blow-up photos were of.

He had found Cheri's kinky cat with the flashlight.

Ballard risked his own flashlight for about thirty seconds. They gave him a queasy feeling, just because there were so many of them. All of the walls, floor to ceiling, scores of them colored, these probably cut from Swedish or German porno magazines, and hundreds of black-and-whites, developed and enlarged in the darkroom downstairs.

Good old Kinky: on these naked girls he had used a camera and a flashbulb instead of a flashlight. Blow-ups, cropped so that only the essential female flesh was left, starkly, crudely exposed.

Kinky indeed. Ballard pulled the door shut behind him, went right down the front stairs to the ground floor. He was glad to be out of the turret room. If only there had been a breast or two depicted, a full nude, above all a face. Even an ugly face, even a Gloria Rouse face. But no. Not for Kinky. For him, the apparently numerous chicks who weren't as selective as buxom, lusty Cheri Tart.

As Ballard opened the cellar door, lights swept the front of the house. He froze. He waited. A car door slammed. He waited some more.

No horn blast from Giselle.

Someone going to a different house, then. It would be a bitch to get trapped in the basement, but the house was empty, and with Giselle on watch he would get at least some warning. But he was glad to have the tire iron in his hand. He turned on the flashlight and went down the steep narrow stairs.

The basement was a mess, the floor loaded with the sort of junk that always seems to accumulate in basements. In one of the front corners a wooden bin which once would have held coal. Above it, a small high window to which the coal chute would have been fitted. An old house indeed. Coal abandoned long ago, of course, for the big natural-gas furnace which dominated the corner of the basement under the kitchen.

Ballard's light jumped nervously about, went by and then suddenly returned to and steadied on a washtub leaned on edge against the wall. There was dried concrete around the edges of the washtub, as if it had been used to mix a small amount of mortar. The light moved again, this time laid its white O on a full bag of Portland cement, with a half-bag set on top of it, upright, with the top scrunched down. Ballard realized that he had not really believed he would find anything down here. Of course, he hadn't found a new section of concrete, but . . .

He found it five minutes later.

It was under some old homemade wooden shelves with two-by-two framing and triple widths of one-by-eight pine planking for shelves. Unpainted, crowded with ranks of antique Mason jars, empty and waiting under their coating of thick dust for the home canning that would never be done. What had caught his eye were the scuff marks made on the floor by the stubby vertical two-by-two legs, as if the shelves had been walked end-for-end out from the wall not too long ago.

Ballard got down on his belly and shone the light under the bottom shelf sagging six inches off the floor. The light, laid flat across the concrete that way, easily picked out the rough join of a rectangle of new concrete with the older, smoother, more professional floor.

Seven feet long. Two feet wide.

Stupid? No. Why would he ever have been suspected? Who would ever come down here to look? And after a few years it wouldn't have looked so raw, so new . . . So here he was, Chuck Griffin, a pretty nice guy by all accounts. He hadn't walked out on Cheri after all. He hadn't embezzled and been murdered for it, either. Murdered, thought Ballard erroneously, to *disguise* an embezzlement he had discovered.

Ballard followed his dancing circle of light up the dusty stairs to the closed door at the top. Time to get out before . . .

Closed door.

He switched off the flashlight abruptly, stood on the stairs in the total blackness, breathing with his mouth open. He had left the door standing open when he had come down, on the theory that it would make it a little easier to hear if Giselle had sounded the horn. But she hadn't. And he'd had the house to himself when he'd come down here. Therefore, he still did. So cool the nerves.

He switched on the light, gingerly climbed the rest of the way. Sure. The door wasn't closed tight, actually; it merely had drifted shut by itself. But it still took a conscious act of will to gently push it open enough to edge an eye out for a quick look down to the front door.

The hall was empty, of course.

Ballard went the rest of the way out of the cellar, started down the hall and froze after two steps.

The front door was ajar.

He could see the thin line of light from the narrow crack, laid across the floor at an angle and standing a few inches up the wall.

The door had been locked when he had tried it from the outside.

But that meant . . .

He heard the grunt of effort and at the same instant

his body arched and he yelled in pure agony as he was slammed in the kidney. The floor came up at him as his mind screamed, through the pain, *He got Giselle first . . .*

Things went away.

Twenty-five

Not entirely away: it had been the sudden intensity of the pain that had made reality go mushy. He realized he was on his hands and knees against the wall. His head hurt as well as his back; must have rammed headfirst into the wall on the way down.

"Blood," he got out. It was the first thing that came to mind. "I'll be pissing blood for a week." He'd read that about kidney injuries in a detective story once.

"Not for a week," said Rodney Elkin in an almost apologetic voice. "I want you to go into the dining room ahead of me. The light switch is to the left of the door."

"I don't know if I can get up," said Ballard. His mind had started to work again, a little. The kidney pain had lessened.

"You'll get up."

He got up. He hiked himself upright against the wall. His eyes were coming back into focus; he could see Elkin standing well away from him, wearing a topcoat. Tall, physically strong, decisive, good-looking, kinky. Especially kinky. Use that some way? The big revolver from the kitchen drawer now in his left hand. Of course. With shells in it now.

Heslip, facing his attacker, had been struck on the right side of his head. Elkin, talking on the phone at JRS Garage, had switched the receiver to his right hand to write notes of the conversation.

"Move it!" snapped Elkin.

Ballard moved it. The gun was shaking in Elkin's hand.

Panic again. Panic might make the gun go off. He used the wall to get to the dining room, leaning against it and sliding along. Go in fast, slam the door, dive out the still-open window . . .

It wasn't like TV, not at all. Away from the wall, he tottered. He hurt. Moving, he had to clench his teeth to keep from throwing up. He couldn't have moved fast if his life depended on it. Christ, his life *did* depend on it!

He still couldn't move fast. He sat down on one of the oak dining chairs, gingerly. Jee*zuz*, that back!

What had Elkin done to Giselle?

Elkin was sweating, holding the gun. Moisture from the fog glistened on his very black, very curly hair. His nose was too big for him to be truly handsome, Ballard thought. So why in hell hadn't Cheri Tart mentioned that nose? Or those extra-long mod sideburns? None of this would have happened if she'd mentioned things like that.

"I don't know what I'm going to do about you, Ballard." He chewed his lip nervously. "I really don't."

"Buy me off."

Elkin gave a short tight laugh full of a sort of despair. He went around drawing the shades, closed the window through which Ballard had entered. He looked like a tennis player, a basketball player, maybe; he didn't look like a murderer. He sat down on the edge of the big oak table, began swinging one leg. His shoes were very brightly polished. His eyes looked sick. "Buy you off with what?"

"The money you embezzled. The money you killed Charles Griffin for—so you could blame him for stealing it."

But Elkin just shook his head, his face almost placid. Ballard suddenly realized: he had to prime himself. Work himself up, as he probably had done with Griffin. As he had done with Bart. As he would do with Larry Ballard unless . . . Would going down on his knees and pleading for his life do any good? Ballard knew he would do it if he thought it would save him.

"I didn't steal any money," said Elkin.

Ballard almost bought it, the way he said it. But if not

for money, then why . . . "Heslip didn't die. He's out of the coma, he can identify you."

That shook Elkin, visibly. He said, "I don't believe you."

"Odum can identify you, too. And Cheri . . ."

His face went pale. "That whore! Don't talk to me about her!"

Use it. Work on it. Mr. Kink. "I saw your trophy room upstairs."

Elkin leaped to his feet, eyes wild. Jesus! Ballard had pushed the wrong button. But now he understood. Everything. Too late he understood it. The furniture had been sold from under Cheri merely to spite her, purely and simply. And Griffin had died, here in this house on February 9, because of Cheri.

As if reading his thoughts, Elkin said, "Chuck was an accident, really." He sank back on the edge of the table; some of the wildness left his eyes. The muzzle of the gun wavered slightly. Ballard would roll suddenly out of the chair, keep rolling, a moving target, then dive right out of the window, shade and curtains and glass and all . . .

Bullshit.

"It *was* an accident. He came over here the night after that bitch over in Concord . . . Anyway, he was accusing me of wild things, things *she'd* said. A cheap whore like that, a topless dancer showing everything she's got to anyone, but when I . . . But . . . Anyway, he . . . he was standing in the living room, by the fireplace, he said . . . He believed what she said about me! He . . . he said if I ever went near her again he . . . he was bigger than I am, a lot heavier, he lifted weights all the time, so I picked up the poker and I hit him. Just to knock him down. But it was turned wrong and . . . the end of it went right into his forehead, right into his skull above his eye. He just fell down dead. An accident . . ."

Where in *hell* was Giselle? Obviously Elkin knew nothing about her. Had she for Christ sake fallen asleep or something in the goddamn car? His back was killing him . . . "So you had to make it look as if Griffin had been embezzling. To explain why he disappeared."

"That's it," he said. His face was working. He transferred the revolver to his right hand, flexed his fingers, returned it to his left. "Since it happened, I've been going down to JRS after supper, some nights, to work on the tallies and receipts to make it look as if he'd been stealing for quite a while."

"On Tuesday you took the W-2 out of Leo's desk after he showed it to Heslip," said Ballard.

"But it was too late. Somehow, from that California Street address, your man got to Odum. On Tuesday night he came by on his way back from the East Bay to tell us what he had learned about Griffin. I was the only one there. After he left I stayed there a while, thinking. I knew Odum had given him a description of Griffin—he kept staring at me while he was there . . ."

"Because the description fit you," said Ballard. "Because you had posed as Griffin to Odum. Why did you? Why San Jose and—"

"What else was I going to do?" he demanded in an aggrieved voice. "I could hide his body in the cellar, but I couldn't put his car down there. I couldn't put it in a JRS Garage, either—someone would have recognized it. So I rented a house down in San Jose, as far away from the city and the East Bay as I could get, and left it in the garage. But then your company came around looking for it."

It was ironic: if he had just left it parked somewhere by Griffin's house, a DKA man would have spotted it, grabbed it, and the investigation would have ended right there. Instead, he had brought in Odum as a way to get rid of it.

"And then Odum didn't keep up the payments," Ballard said.

"And here you are." His voice had roughened, coarsened, deepened. Working himself up to it? No. Please . . . "You had to keep going. You wouldn't let me alone."

Oh Jesus Christ, this was it. It *couldn't* be, he was only twenty-six years old, he couldn't die yet, Jesus, he was going to shit his pants or something . . .

Elkin took a deep breath. His hand raised the heavy revolver.

And the front door slammed.

The gun muzzle wavered. Elkin's face had become frantic with indecision. When whoever it was came through the door, Ballard would lunge for the bourbon bottle on the sideboard, throw it . . .

Heavy careless footsteps tramping down the hall, heavy as doom. Elkin whispered furiously at Ballard as if they were fellow conspirators, *"Who . . ."*

A hard-faced, compact, bleak-eyed man in a dark topcoat came through the door, stopped. His hands were in his coat pockets. Elkin swung the muzzle of the revolver toward him, but the man was unaffected. His eyes went from one of them to the other and back. Ballard was on his feet.

"Rodney Elkin?" said the hard-faced man.

"I'm . . . Elkin." The gun was wavering; he didn't know who to point it at. If Ballard had been himself he could have taken him then. He didn't even try.

"Inspector Ed Gough, Homicide, SFPD," said the bleak-eyed man. Ballard had a sudden totally irrational urge to start laughing. "You are under arrest for the murder of Charles M. Griffin on the night of Wednesday, February ninth. You have the right to remain silent. You have the right to counsel. If you cannot afford an attorney, the court will appoint one for you. If you choose—"

"But . . . I have a gun!" exclaimed Elkin. He had gone into an oddly theatrical half-crouch, like a Western gunfighter on a Hollywood sound studio street.

"So do I," said Gough. "And I know how to use mine." He looked over at Ballard as if Elkin's revolver did not exist. "Who the hell are you?"

"La . . . Larry Ballard," he said in a carefully controlled voice.

"You a friend of his?"

"Private investigator."

"Give me your belt," said Gough.

"I have a gun!" yelled Elkin. He looked as if he wanted

to cry; all three of them, oddly, knew that the time he could have used it had already passed.

"Don't make me take it away from you, sonny. We've had a police accountant going through the books at JRS two nights a week since sometime in April. Spectographic analysis of the inks in the ledgers show some entries were altered, others put in at different times since Griffin was murdered, trying to make it look as if the entries predated his disappearance. We've got an eyeball witness to Griffin coming to this house on February ninth. We've got an eyeball of you at the San Jose house in March. We've got an eyeball of someone answering your description putting a black man into a Jaguar on Golden Gate Avenue at one-fifteen A.M. on Wednesday morning. The witness got a partial make on the license plate. Should I go on?"

The three men stood looking at one another with a strange intimacy in the unused dining room. Finally Elkin gave a little sob and laid the revolver on the oak table. His hands were shaking so badly that the steel clattered against the wood. He no longer looked like an athlete: he was just a lanky, frightened man with a nose that was big enough to keep him from being truly handsome.

Gough stepped forward, scooped up the revolver, dropped it into a coat pocket. "Turn around," he said. Elkin did. Gough made impatient gestures at Ballard. "Your belt. I got roped into a big drug bust down in the Haight on the way up here, I don't have any cuffs with me."

Ballard gave him the belt. Ballard's face ached from being kept impassive. As Gough lashed Elkin's hands behind him, the faint far wail of a siren came from down toward Stanyan. Gough nodded.

"That'll be a prowl car." He grabbed the tall murderer's shoulder in an ungentle grip. "Let's go. We'll meet them out in front."

Ballard followed them to the front door. The fog had thinned; as they went down the front walk, Giselle's tall golden-haired form appeared on the sidewalk. Gough went by her without a glance; she turned and stared after him as if she had never seen a cop before. Then she burst out laughing.

"Where the hell have you been?" Ballard yelled at her.

Giselle quit laughing and ran up the walk. "Larry! Are you all right?"

He put a hand to his kidney and groaned. Actually, it didn't feel too bad; but he had to go to the bathroom and was afraid to. If blood came out . . . "I was almost killed!" he exclaimed. "Why in hell didn't you blow the horn when Elkin showed up?"

She gestured after Ed Gough. "He got in the car with me about fifteen minutes after you left. He'd had the same idea as you, to search for the body. But since you were already inside, he said let you find it. But then Elkin showed up. He told me to run for a phone, and then he followed Elkin right up the walk and into the house. No gun, no nothing. He looked awfully damned good doing it, Larry."

So the bastard had been in the house when Ballard had been attacked, probably had been hiding out of sight at the foot of the stairs to the second floor, just inside the front door. Had let Ballard get slammed in the kidneys and hadn't done a damned thing. Had then slammed the front door from the inside and come down the hall at the crucial moment.

An SFPD radio unit squealed into Java from Masonic, red lights turning, siren dying. Two uniformed cops jumped out.

Ballard turned and started down the hall. "There's a bottle of bourbon in the dining room."

Ten minutes later the front door slammed and familiar aggressive footsteps came down the hall.

"How did you know Elkin was the one?" demanded Ballard as Dan Kearny alias Ed Gough came into the room.

"When I was driving back in the T-Bird," said Kearny, "I realized Griffin seemed to be *two men*—one who attacked Bart coldly and viciously, the other who was Cheri's gentle soul drinking too much out of grief about his mother's death. Then I finally caught on that *some-*

where along the line a substitution had been made, a phony for a real Griffin. It had to be after Cheri and before Odum. So . . ."

"So," said Giselle, "as soon as you realized you had two different psychological descriptions, you started looking for two different physical descriptions, right?"

"I finally started to *think* about the evidence instead of just walk around it. When I did that, Elkin stuck out like a broken thumb. Only he talked with Griffin when Griffin called in sick on the tenth and eleventh of February. He was the one who started the talk that Griffin might have been embezzling. He was the one who told Larry that Griffin had said the mother's will was out of probate —nobody else heard Griffin say that. He fit Cheri's description of Griffin's kinky friend. Even getting rid of the furniture in the California Street house—if that *wasn't* Griffin, it had to be somebody who knew Griffin wouldn't be around to object. So then I went back and asked Odum the two questions I should have asked him in the first place."

"For a description of Griffin," said Ballard. "But what was the second?"

"Whether Odum gave the description to Bart. He did."

"And Bart caught up with the description on the wrong person. He thought it was just a coincidence, but he wanted to ask me about it because it bothered him."

"Well," said Giselle. She looked at her watch, but said, "What's the penalty for impersonating a police officer, Dan?"

Kearny stopped at the door, grinned. He had to get down to Fifth and Bryant to sign the murder complaint against Elkin so he could be held without bail. "I liked the stuff about the spectographic analysis of inks, myself. You ought to get out of here if you don't want to get stuck for the rest of the night. They'll be coming with a warrant to bust up that cellar floor. Damned good job, you two. Take the day off."

"It's Saturday," said Giselle. "We aren't supposed to work anyway."

"Then take Sunday off, too."

"Why didn't you call yourself Joe Friday?" asked Ballard coldly.

"You know I always use street names for my aliases," said Kearny with great dignity. "Bush. Franklin. Turk. Gough. One of these days I'll have to work something up with Golden Gate in it."

They stared at the empty doorway, listened to Kearny's energetic footsteps pound back down the hall. The front door slammed.

Ballard shook his head in wonder. "The son of a bitch probably will, too."

Giselle laughed. Then she said, "Looks like you're stuck with running me over to Oakland after all."

Ballard used a four-letter word. Then, gritting his teeth, he used Elkin's bathroom. No blood. Which cheered him so much that he took the bottle of bourbon with him. Maybe he could sneak it into the hospital in the morning. Bart liked bourbon, and Corinne Jones would take a sip of it from time to time. Especially when she had something to celebrate.

About the Author

JOE GORES spent twelve years as a private investigator in San Francisco—an experience which makes *Dead Skip* as real as a tapped phone. He holds degrees in English literature from Notre Dame and Stanford, and has lived in such exotic places as Tahiti, Kenya and the Seychelles. He has taught school in East Africa, has logged in Alaska, has managed a "hot sheet" motel and a weight-lifting gym. In 1970 he became the first dual Edgar-winner in Mystery Writers of America history—for his first novel, *A Time of Predators,* and for the short story "Goodbye, Pops." His work, including an exhaustive maritime history, *Marine Salvage,* and over a hundred short stories, has been translated into nine languages. Currently living in San Francisco with his wife, Susan, he is working on novels, screen plays and short fiction.

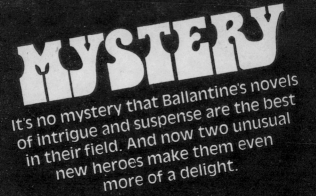